Mefisto

JOHN BANVILLE was born in Wexford, Ireland, in 1945.
He is the author of fourteen other novels including
The Sea, which won the 2005 Man Booker Prize.
He has received a literary award from the
Lannan Foundation. He lives in Dublin.

JOHN BANVILLE

Mefisto

PICADOR

First published 1986 by Martin Secker & Warburg Limited

First published by Picador 1999
an imprint of Pan Macmillan, a division of Macmillan Publishers Limited
Pan Macmillan, 20 New Wharf Road, London N1 9RR
Basingstoke and Oxford
Associated companies throughout the world
www.panmacmillan.com

ISBN 978-0-330-37231-2

3 5 7 9 8 6 4

A CIP catalogue record for this book is available from
the British Library.

Printed in the UK by CPI Mackays, Chatham ME5 8TD

to Janet

I

MARIONETTES

CHANCE WAS IN the beginning. I am thinking of that tiny swimmer, alone of all its kind, surging in frantic ardour towards the burning town, the white room and Castor dead. Strange, that a life so taken up with the swell and swarm of numbers should start, like a flourish between mirrors, in the banal mathematics of gemination. The end also was chance.

There was a Polydeuces too, of course. Who only is escaped alone etcetera.

We were not the first, of our kind, in our tribe. On my mother's side there had been another pair, monovular also, though they both perished, their lives a brief day. Pity they weren't bottled, I could have them for a mascot, my translucent little grand-uncles, fists clenched, frowning in their fluid. There is too a more subtle echo in the symmetrical arrangement of grandparents, Jack Kay and Grandfather Swan and their miniature wives. Thus the world slyly nudges us, showing up the seemingly random for what it really is. I could go on. I shall go on.

I too have my equations, my symmetries, and will insist on them.

When did my mother realize the nature of the cargo she was carrying? What archangel spoke? Dualities perhaps would fascinate her, glimpsed reflections, coincidences of course. A pair of magpies swaggering among the cabbages gave her a fright. Old sayings might strike her with a new significance: peas in a pod, two new pins, chalk and cheese. Maybe now and then she fancied she could hear us, horribly together in our crowded amniotic sea, crooning and tinily crying.

She was herself undergoing a kind of gemination. Her condition did not so much change her as produce another person. Her ankles swelled, her hips thickened. Even her shoulders seemed broader, packed with soft flesh. She began to wear her hair pulled back in two tight, gleaming black wings and tied at the nape in a netted bun. When she went out to Ashburn, Jack Kay gazed at her mournfully and said:

– Where is my girl gone, my little girl?

She looked at him askance, unsmiling, and for an instant clearly he saw his own mother. He shook his great grizzled head.

– Pah! he said sourly, you're a woman now.

I picture her, in that last springtime of the war. Mine is yet another version of her, not the mother she was becoming, nor the daughter Jack Kay had lost, but a stranger, silent and enigmatic, disconsolately smiling, like a dark madonna in the brownish sea-light of some old painting. The burden she carries under her heart weighs on her like a weight of sadness. She had not asked for this outlandish visitation. She begins to feel a secret revulsion. Blood, torn flesh, the gaping lips of a cut before the seepage starts, such things have always appalled her. In the butcher's shop she cannot look at the strung-up waxen flanks of meat surreptitiously dripping pink syrup on the sawdust floor. She feels like a walking bruise, fevered and tumescent. Certain smells sicken her, of cooked cabbage, coal tar, leather. Images lodge in her head, anything will do, a cracked egg, a soiled dishrag, as if her mind is desperate for things with which to torment her. She cannot sleep.

– I'm not well. I don't feel well.

– You must pray, child.

His eyes glint behind the grille, his teeth seem bared in a smiling grimace. She can smell the altar wine on his breath.

– I'm afraid.

– What's that?

– I'm afraid, father.

– Oh now. Ask the Blessed Virgin to help you.

Everything crowds in on her. Her parents are evicted from the cottage at Ashburn, and move in with her. Her mother, already limbering up for death, soon fades into the county hospital. Jack Kay remains. He paces the house silently, looking at her out of tragic eyes, as if somehow everything were her fault.

She cannot be still. She is suffocating. She takes long, aimless walks, dragging herself through the town and out along the Coolmine road, by the rubbish dump. One day a crow falls down dead out of a tree on her head. She does not know whether to laugh or scream. For weeks she will keep hearing the sudden thump, the crackle of feathers, and feel the limp, blue-black thing sliding down her front. The summer is hot. Europe is in ruins. She straggles home, and finds Jack Kay sitting on the window-sill beside the front door, swinging one leg, his big white hands folded on the crook of his stick. She says:

– The key is there.

– Key, what key? I don't know about any key.

– There! It's always there!

He looks on mildly as she snatches up the doormat furiously and points. An agile beetle scuttles for safety. She crushes the key into the lock. Dank air in the hall, and a sullen silence as of things interrupted at furtive play. She begins to say something, but stops, catching her breath. Jack Kay, purblind in the gloom, almost collides with her, and steps back with a grunt. She is leaning against the wall, holding herself. When she turns to the light from the doorway her face is ashen, with a sheen of sweat.

– Go get someone, she whispers. Quick!

He opens his mouth and shuts it again.

The sumptuous light of summer fills the bedroom. A lace curtain billows lazily in the wide-open window. It all seems so heartless. She thrashes slowly on the bed, shielding her face in her arms, as if trapped beneath a press of forms fighting in silent ferocity. Jack Kay has followed her up, and stands now in the doorway, goggling.

– Get out! she cries. Get out!

THE BOOKSHELLF

QTY DEPT	DESCRIPTION	@ PRICE DIS%
1 C007	MEMBERSHIP FA	25.00	p
1 A018	BOOK - REMAIN	7.99	10.0 p
1 A018	BOOK - REMAIN	7.99	10.0 p

```
                    GROSS SALE:      40.98
                    DISCOUNT:        -1.60
          3         NET SALE:        39.38

HST#: R105198246   HST:              3.97
                   GRAND TOTAL:      43.35

                   PAYMENT: VISA     43.35
                   CHANGE DUE:        0.00
```

She understands at last what it means that the thing inside her is alive, alive.

Jack Kay descended the stairs, stopping at every third step to look back at the bedroom door, muttering. It was not right she should shout at him like that, like a madwoman. He opened the front door cautiously. An ordinary afternoon in summer. He listened a moment, then stepped outside and closed the door behind him, holding the flap with his heel and letting it down quietly. *Go get someone*, he mouthed, wagging his head, *quick quick*! He spat. A dog approached him. He lifted his stick and the animal cringed, licking thin lips. The stick was a comfortable weight in his hand, good stout malacca worn to the texture of wax, with a hallmarked silver band and a steel ferrule. He frowned, trying to recall when or where he had come by it. He thought briefly of death, then tipped the brim of his hat over one eye and sauntered off across the square. And did not hear the cry that issued from the open upstairs window behind him, nor the second, weaker wail, that wavered, and sank, like a tiny hand going under.

I DON'T KNOW when it was that I first heard of the existence, if that's the word, of my dead brother. From the start I knew I was the survivor of some small catastrophe, the shock-waves were still reverberating faintly inside me. The mysterious phenomenon that produced us is the result, the textbooks tell me, of a minor arrest in the early development of a single egg, so that the embryonic streak begins dividing by binary fission. I prefer to picture something like a scene from a naughty seaside postcard, the fat lady, apple cheeks, big bubs and mighty buttocks, cloven clean in two by her driven little consort. However, the cause is no matter, only the effect. The perils we had missed were many. We might have been siamese. One of us might have exsanguinated into the other's circulation. Or we might simply have strangled one another. All this we escaped, and surfaced at last, gasping. I came first. My brother was a poor second. Spent swimmer, he drowned in air. My father, when Jack Kay fetched him home at last, looked in dull wonderment at the scene: the infant mewling

8

in its mother's arms, and that lifeless replica of it laid out on the sheet.

My mother feared I too would die. Jack Kay reminded her how his brothers, her homuncles, had succumbed after a day. She nursed me with a kind of vehemence, willing me to live. She would not let me out of her sight. She made a nest for me in the big drawer of the wardrobe in her bedroom. I see myself lying there, unnaturally silent, slowly flexing my bandy arms and legs, like a tortoise stranded on its back. When she leans over me I look at her gropingly and frown. My vague, bleached gaze is that of a traveller come back from somewhere immensely far and strange. At night she lay awake and listened to the furtive noises this new life made, the shufflings and soft sighs, and now and then what sounded like a muffled exclamation of impatience. Later on, when I had learned to walk, and could get away by myself, I developed a private language, a rapid, aquatic burbling, which made people uneasy. It sounded as if I were conversing with someone. Hearing me, my mother would pause outside my door, on the stairs, and I in turn, hearing her, would immediately fall silent. Thus we would remain, the two of us, for a long time, alert, motionless, listening to our own inexplicably palpitant heartbeats. Jack Kay, moustache twitching, wondered aloud if maybe I was wrong in the head.

I feel a tender, retrospective concern, mixed with a trace of contempt, it's true, for this baffled little boy who moves through my memories of those first years in watchful solitude, warily. I clung to the house. My bedroom looked down through two tiny windows into the square, it was like hiding inside a head. I seemed to myself not whole, nor

9

wholly real. Fairytales fascinated me, there was something dismayingly familiar in them, the mad logic, the discontinuities, the random cruelty of fate. I was brought to a circus, I remember it, the noise, the flashing lights, the brass farts of the band, the incongruous scent of crushed grass coming up between the seats. There were tumbling midgets, and a woman with a snake, and a brilliantined contortionist, thin as a blade, who sat down on his coccyx and assembled a series of agonized tableaux with the stony detachment of a pornographer displaying his wares. It was the clowns, though, that really unnerved me, with their pointy heads and rubber feet and oddly diffused yells, the way they kept tormenting each other, the way the short one would stand bawling in frustration and seeming pain and then whirl round suddenly and smash his lanky companion full in the face with terrible, steely insouciance. I sat without a stir throughout the show, gazing down into the lighted ring with wistful avidity, like that boy in the story who longed to learn how to shudder.

My mother took me for walks, first in a pram, then tottering ahead of her on a sort of reins, then dawdling farther and farther behind her along the hedgerows. Sometimes we went as far as Ashburn and wandered through the unkempt grounds. She showed me the cottage where she was born, behind the stables. Ashburn would be for her always an idyll. The life of the big house, at the far fringes of which she had hovered longingly, she remembered as a languorous mime to the music of tick-tocking tennis balls across green lawns and the far-off bleat of the huntsman's horn on frosty mornings, a scene small and distant, yet perfectly, preciously detailed, atinkle with tiny laughter, like a picture glimpsed of eighteenth-century aristocrats at play in a dappled glade. In the midst of this pretty pastoral stood the cottage, where the frog king Jack Kay had reigned. Here her memories were more precise, of whitewash, and rats in the thatch, the tin bath in front of the fire on Saturday nights, a speckled hen standing on one leg in a patch of sun in the kitchen doorway. And the endless squabbles, of course, the shouting, the boxed ears. Now the stables were falling, the forge where Jack Kay had worked was silent. One day, on an overgrown path, under a huge tree, we met Miss Kitty, the last of the Ashburns of Ashburn Park, a distracted and not very clean maiden lady with a great beaked nose and tangled hair, who talked to us calmly enough for a bit, then turned abruptly and ordered us off the estate, waving her arms and shouting.

There were other spectacles, other frights. I have only a single recollection of Grandfather Swan, a big effigy sitting up in bed laughing in the little house in Queen Street. It was Easter morning, and I was five years old. The sick-room smelled of pipe tobacco and piss. There was a window open beside the bed. The sunlight outside glittered after a recent shower. Grandfather Swan had been shaving, the bowl and cut-throat and bit of looking-glass were still beside him, and there was a fleck of fresh blood on the collar of his nightshirt. His hands trembled, apart from that he seemed quite hale. But he was dying. I was conscious of the solemnity of the occasion. Hard fingers prodded me between the shoulder-blades, and I stepped forward, gazing in awe at the old man's taut white brow and big moustache, the agate nails, the swept-back spikes of iron-grey hair that made it seem as if some force were dragging the head away and up, to the window, to the shining roofs, to the spring sky itself, pale blue and chill like his eyes. He must have talked to me, but I remember only his laugh, not so much a sound as something that surrounded him, like an aura, and not at all benign. For a long time death was to seem a sort of disembodied, sinister merriment sitting in wait for me in that fetid little room.

And yet, I wonder. Is this really a picture of Grandfather Swan, or did I in my imagination that Easter morn wishfully substitute another, tougher old man for this one who was doomed? I mean Jack Kay. The laugh, the alarming fingernails, the wirebrush moustache stained yellow in the middle, all these are his, surely? Jack Kay. To me he was always eighty. He wore his years like a badge of tenacity, grimly, with a kind of truculence. But let me have done with him. He lived at Ashburn, and worked the forge. He was an intermittent drunkard. He married Martha somebody, I forget the name, a scullery maid at the big house. They had children. They were unhappy.

Or at least Martha was. I do not see her clearly. She and Granny Swan died about the same time. They blur into each other, two put-upon old women, somehow not quite life-sized, dropsical, dressed in black, always unwell, always complaining. Their voices are a faint, background murmur, like the twittering of mice behind a wainscot. They must have had some effect, must have contributed a gene or two, yet there remains almost nothing of them. In the matter of heredity they were no match for their menfolk. All the same, there is a memory, which, though neither woman is really in it, is their inspiration. One of those windy damp days of early autumn, with a sky of low, dove-grey cloud, the shining pavements plastered with leaves, and an empty dustbin rolling on its side in the middle of the road. Someone had told me my granny was dead. The news, far from being sad, was strangely exhilarating, and there on that street suddenly I was filled with a snug excitement, which I could not explain, but which was somehow to do with life, with the future. I was not thinking of the living woman, she had been of scant significance to me. In death, however, she had become one with those secret touchstones the thought of which comforted and mysteriously sustained me: small lost animals, the picturesque poor, warnings of gales at sea, the naked feet of Franciscans.

I don't know which of the two women it was that had died. Let the image of that silvery light on that rainy road be a memorial, however paltry, to them both.

My father in these early memories is a remote, enigmatic and yet peculiarly vivid figure. He worked as a tallyman for a grain merchant. He smelled of chaff, dust, jute, all dry things. He had asthma, and a bad leg. His silences, into which a remark about the weather or a threat of death would drop alike without trace, were a force in our house, like a dull drumming that has gone on for so long it has ceased to be heard but is still vaguely, disturbingly felt. His presence, diffident and fleeting, lent a mysterious weight to the most trivial occasion. He took me to the Fort mountain one day on the bar of his bicycle. It was September, clear and still. The heather was in bloom. We sat on a ditch eating sandwiches, and drinking tepid milk out of lemonade bottles that my mother had filled for us and corked with twists of paper. The sanatorium was high up behind us, hidden among pines except for the steep-pitched roof and a tall cluster of chimneys, closed, silent, alluring. I toyed dreamily with the thought of myself reclining in a timeless swoon on the veranda up there, swaddled in blankets, with the dazzling white building at my back and the sun slowly falling down the sky in front of me, and a wireless somewhere quietly playing danceband music. My father wore a flat cap and a heavy, square-cut overcoat, a size too big for him, that smelled of mothballs. He pointed out a hawk wheeling in the zenith.

– Take the eye out of you, he said, one of them lads.

He was a short man, with long arms and bowed legs. His head was small, which made his trunk seem weightier than it was. With those limbs, that sharp face, the close-set dark eyes, he had something of those stunted little warriors, the dark-haired ones, Pict or Firbolg, I don't know, who stalk the far borders of history. I can see him, in pelts and pointed shoon, limping at twilight through the bracken. A small man, whom the vengeful gods have overlooked. A survivor.

Sometimes I catch myself dreaming that dream in which childhood is an endless festival, with bands of blond children sweeping through the streets in sunlight, laughing. I can almost see the tunics, the sandalled feet, the white-robed elders watching indulgently from the olive tree's shade. Something must have fed this Attic fantasy, a game of tag, perhaps, on a Sunday evening in summer, the houses open to the tender air, and mothers on the doorsteps, talking, and someone's sister, in her first lipstick, leaning at gaze out of an upstairs window.

The town was twelve thousand souls, three churches and a Methodist hall, a narrow main street, a disused anthracite mine, a river and a silted harbour. Fragments of the past stuck up through the present, rocks in the stream of time: a Viking burial mound, a Norman tower, a stump of immemorial wall like a broken molar. History was rich there. Giraldus Cambrensis knew that shore. The Templars had kept a hospice on the Spike peninsula. The region had played its part in more than one failed uprising. By now the splendour had faded. There was too, I almost forgot, the great war against the Jehovah's Witnesses, I had watched the final rout: a priest punching in the belly a skinny young man in a mac, the crowd shouting, the bundles of *The Watchtower* flying in the air. And there was a celebrated murder, never solved, an old woman battered to death one dark night in her sweetshop down a lane. It was the stuff of nightmares, the body behind the counter, the bottled sweets, the blood.

A picture of the town hangs in my mind, like one of those priceless yet not much prized medieval miniatures, its provenance uncertain, its symbols no longer quite explicable, the translucency of its faded colours lending it a quaint, accidental charm. Can it really all be so long ago, so different, or is this antique tawny patina only the varnish which memory applies even to a recent past? It's true, there is a lacquered quality to the light of those remembered days. The grey of a wet afternoon in winter would be the aptest shade, yet I think of a grocer's brass scales standing in a beam of dusty sunlight, a bit of smooth blue china – they were called chaynies – found in the garden and kept for years, and there blooms before my inward gaze the glow of pale gold wings in a pellucid, Limbourg-blue sky.

Along with the tower and the broken wall there were the human antiquities, the maimed and the mad, the hunchbacks, the frantic old crones in their bonnets and black coats, and the mongols, with their little eyes and bad feet and sweet smiles, gambolling at the heels of touchingly middle-aged mothers. They were all of them a sort of brotherhood, in which I was a mere acolyte. It had its high priests too. There was the little man who came one summer to stay with relatives on the other side of our square. He wore blue suits and shiny shoes, pearl cufflinks, a ruby ring. He had a large handsome head and a barrel chest. His hair was a masterpiece, black and smooth as shellac, as if a gramophone record had been moulded to his skull. He rode an outsize tricycle. Astride this machine he held court under the trees of the square, surrounded by a mesmerized crowd of children, his arms folded and one gleaming toecap touching the ground with balletic delicacy. He was in a way the ideal adult, bejewelled, primped and pomaded, magisterially self-possessed, and just four feet tall. His manners were exquisite. Such tact! In his presence I felt hardly different from ordinary children.

I went to the convent school. Corridors painted a light shade of sick, tall windows with sash cords taut as a noose, and nuns, a species of large black raptor, swooping through the classrooms, their rosaries clacking like jesses. I feared my classmates, and despised them too. I can see them still, their gargoyle faces, the kiss curls, the snot. My name for some reason they found funny. They would bring their brothers or their big sisters to confront me in the playground.

– There he is, ask him.

– You, what's your name?

– Nobody.

– Come on, say it!

And they would get me by the scruff.

– Gabriel . . . ow! . . . Gabriel Swan.

It sent them into fits, it never failed.

In my class there was another pair of, yes, of identical twins, listless little fellows with pale eyes and knobbly, defenceless knees. I was fascinated. They were so calm, so unconcerned, as if being alike were a trick they had mastered long ago, and thought nothing of any more. They could have had such a time, playing pranks, switching places, fooling everybody. That was what fascinated me, the thought of being able to escape effortlessly, as if by magic, into another name, another self – that, and the ease too with which they could assert their separate identities, simply by walking away from each other. Apart, each twin was himself. Only together were they a freak.

But I, I had something always beside me. It was not a presence, but a momentous absence. From it there was no escape. A connecting cord remained, which parturition and even death had not broken, along which by subtle tugs and thrums I sensed what was not there. No living double could have been so tenacious as this dead one. Emptiness weighed on me. It seemed to me I was not all my own, that I was being shared. If I fell, say, and cut my knee, I would be aware immediately of an echo, a kind of chime, as of a wine-glass shattering somewhere out of sight, and I would feel a soft shock like that when the dreamer on the brink of blackness puts a foot on a step which is not there. Perhaps the pain was lessened – how would I have known?

Sometimes this sense of being burdened, of being somehow imposed upon, gave way to a vague and seemingly objectless yearning. One wet afternoon, at the home of a friend of my mother's who was a midwife, I got my hands on a manual of obstetrics which I pored over hotly for five tingling minutes, quaking in excitement and fear at all this amazing new knowledge. It was not, however, the gynaecological surprises that held me, slack-jawed and softly panting, as if I had stumbled on the most entrancing erotica, but that section of glossy, rubensesque colour plates depicting some of mother nature's more lavish mistakes, the scrambled blastomeres, the androgynes welded at hip or breast, the bicipitous monsters with tiny webbed hands and cloven spines, all those queer, inseverable things among which I and my phantom brother might have been one more.

It seems out of all this somehow that my gift for numbers grew. From the beginning, I suppose, I was obsessed with the mystery of the unit, and everything else followed. Even yet I cannot see a one and a zero juxtaposed without feeling deep within me the vibration of a dark, answering note. Before I could talk I had been able to count, laying out my building blocks in ranked squares, screaming if anyone dared to disturb them. I remember a toy abacus that I treasured for years, with multicoloured wooden beads, and a wooden frame, and little carved feet for it to stand on. My party piece was to add up large numbers instantly in my head, frowning, a hand to my brow, my eyes downcast. It was not the manipulation of things that pleased me, the mere facility, but the sense of order I felt, of harmony, of symmetry and completeness.

S T   S T E P H E N ' S   S C H O O L stood on a hill in the middle of the town, a tall, narrow, red-brick building with a black slate roof and a tin weathercock. I think of damp flagstones and the crash of boots, rain in the yard, and the smell of drains, and something else, a sense of enclosure, of faces averted from the world in holy fright. On my first day there I sat with the other new boys in solemn silence while a red-haired master reached into an immensely deep pocket and brought out lovingly a leather strap.

– Say hello, he said, to teacher's pet.

The thing lolled in his hand like a parched and blackened tongue. Each boy could hear his neighbour swallow. Suddenly all of life up to this seemed a heedless, half-drunk frolic. Outside the window there was a stricken tree, then a field, then firs, then the hurt blue of a bare September sky.

I sat at the front of the class, appalled and fascinated. Each master, even the mildest, seemed mad in his own way. All were convinced that plots were being hatched behind their backs. They would whirl round on a heel from the blackboard, chalk suspended, and fix one boy or another wordlessly with a stare of smouldering suspicion. Without warning they would fly into terrible rages, diving among the desks after a miscreant and raining down blows on him as on some blunt obstruction against which they had barked their shins. Afterwards they were all shamefaced bluster, while the rest of the class averted its gaze from the victim slumped at his desk, hiccuping softly and knuckling his eyes.

At first I tried placating these distraught, violent men, offering up to them my skill at sums, tentatively, like a little gift. They were strangely unimpressed, indignant even, as if they thought it was all a trick, a form of conjuring, gaudy and shallow. I puzzled them, I suppose. I could do all sorts of mental calculations, yet the simplest things baffled me. Dates I found especially slippery. I was never sure what age I was, not knowing exactly what to subtract from what, since my first birthday had fallen not in the year in which I was born, but in the following year, and since, halfway through the present year, when another birthday arrived, I would find myself suddenly a year older, with half a year still to run on the calendar. It all had too much of actuality sticking to it. I felt at ease only with pure numbers, if a sum had solid things in it I balked, like a hamfisted juggler, bobbing and ducking frantically as half-crowns and cabbages, dominoes and sixpences, whizzed out of control around my head. And then there were those exemplars, those faceless men, measuring out the miles from A to B and from B to C, each at his own unwavering pace, I saw them in my mind, solitary, driven, labouring along white roads, in vast, white light. These things, these whizzing objects and tireless striding figures, plucked thus out of humble obscurity, had about them an air of startlement and gathering alarm with which I sympathized. They had never expected to be so intensely noticed.

– Well, Swan, how many apples does that make, eh?

A ripe red shape, with a sunburst trembling on its polished cheek, swelled and swelled in my brain, forcing out everything else.

– You are a dolt, my man. What are you?

– A dolt, sir.

– Precisely! Now put out your hand.

I would not cry, no matter how hard they hit me. I would sit with teeth clenched, my humming palms pressed between my knees and the blood slowly draining out of my face, and sometimes then, gratifyingly, it would seem the master, not I, who had suffered the worse humiliation.

Yet I did well, despite everything. I came top of the class. Every year I won the school prize for mental arithmetic. At home I kept such things dark. On the last day of every summer term, I would stop at the sluice gate behind the malt store on my way home, and tear up my report card and scatter the pieces on the surge.

Then without warning I was summoned one day to the headmaster's office. My mother was there, in hat and Sunday coat, with her bag on her knees and her hands on her bag, motionless, looking at the carpet. The room was cramped and dim. On a pedestal on the wall a statue of a consumptive Virgin stood with heart transpierced, her little hands held out in a lugubrious gesture. It was a spring day outside, windy and bright. Father Barker's big feet stuck out from under his desk, shod in lace-up black boots with thickly mended soles, and uppers worn to the texture of black crape paper. He was a large unhappy man with a moon face, blue-jowled and ponderous of gait. His nickname was Hound. This is a bit-part. He rose, delving under the skirts of his soutane, and brought out a grubby packet of cigarettes. He smoked with a kind of violence, grimly, as if performing an irksome but unavoidable duty. He had been saying, he said, what a fine scholar I was. He came from behind the desk and paced to and fro, his soutane swinging. At each turn he swerved heavily, like a horseman hauling an awkward mount. Grey worms of ash tumbled down the shiny black slope of his belly. He had high hopes, he said. He stopped, and loomed at my mother earnestly.

– High hopes, ma'am!

She lifted her gaze to me at last, reproachful, mute, a minor conspirator who has just found out the enormity of the plot. I looked away from her, to the window and the bright, blown day. Far trees heaved in silence, hugely labouring. I said nothing. Father Barker, lighting up again, was swallowed in a swirl of smoke and flying sparks.

Later, when I came home, a terrible silence reigned in the house. My mother stalked about the kitchen, still wearing her hat, buffeted by a storm of emotions, anger and pride, vague dread, a baffled resentment.

– Like a fool, I was, she cried. Like a fool, sitting there!

She had a horror of being singled out.

In the senior school our mathematics master was a man called Pender. He was English, and a layman. How he had come to St Stephen's no one seemed to know. Elderly, thin, with a narrow, wedge-shaped head and long, curved limbs, he moved with the slow stealth of some tree-climbing creature. His suits, of good broadcloth greased with age, had the loose, crumpled look of a skin about to be sloughed. His taste was for the byways and blind alleys of his subject, for paradoxes and puzzles and mathematical games. He introduced into his lessons the most outlandish things, curved geometries and strange algebras, and strange ways of numbering. I can still recite a litany of the queer names I first heard in his class: Minkowski and Euler, Peano and Heaviside, Infeld, Sperner, Tarski and Olbers. He liked to bewilder his pupils, it was a form of tyranny. He would circle the room at a slow prance, his long arms intricately folded, surveying with a sardonic grin the rows of faces lifted up to him in attentive blankness. Common words when he spoke them – set, system, transformation, braid – took on an almost religious significance. He had a liturgical aspect himself, when he stood by the window, his profile lifted to the day's pale light, a halo of white hair aglow on his gleaming pate, and spoke in his thin, piping voice of the binomial theorem, or boolean algebra, or of the mysterious affinity between the numbers of a fibonacci sequence and the spiral pattern of seeds on the face of a sunflower.

He was delighted with me, of course, but wary too, as if he suspected a trap. He tiptoed around me with nervous jocularity, swooping down on me suddenly as if to grab me, the wattles of his scrawny neck wobbling, and then quickly drawing back again, with a hissing laugh, darting a grey tongue-tip through a gap in his teeth where an eye-tooth was missing. By now I knew differential calculus, could solve the most delicate problems in trigonometry.

– Amazing, Mr Pender would sigh, chafing his papery hands. Quite amazing!

And he would laugh, his thin lips curling in a kind of snarl and the tip of his tongue darting out.

The class began to call me Pender's pet. But I did not welcome this cloying and somehow perilous connection. The beatings that I used to get were less embarrassing, less difficult to manage, than Mr Pender's furtive patronage. I tried retreating from him, made deliberate mistakes, pretended bafflement, but he saw through me, and smiled, with pursed mouth and cocked eyebrow, and pinched the back of my neck, and passed on blandly to other things.

Then one afternoon he appeared unannounced at our house. He sported a louche felt hat and carried a cane. Away from school he had the raffish, edgy air of an out-of-work actor.

– Mrs Swan? I was passing, and . . .

He smiled. She backed away from him, wiping her hands on her apron. Our square, she knew, was not a part of town Mr Pender would find himself in by chance. Sudden strangers worried her. She put him in the parlour and gave him a glass of sherry, bearing the thimble of tawny syrup from the sideboard with tremulous care.

– Ah, so kind.

She stood as in a trance, her hands clasped, not looking at him directly, but absorbing him in bits, his hat, his slender fingers, the limp bow-tie. He spoke quietly, with intensity, his eyes fixed on the table. She hardly listened, captivated by his delicate, attenuated presence. She had an urge to touch him. He sat, one narrow knee crossed on the other, fingering the stem of his glass. He had the faintly sinister self-possession of a priceless piece among fakes. Around him the familiar succumbed to a dispiriting magic. The flowered carpet, the wrought-iron firescreen, the plaster ducks ascending the wall, these things would never be the same again.

– An extraordinary phenomenon, Mrs Swan. Such a brilliant gift. A miracle, really. What can I say? One feels privileged.

An eager light glowed in his glaucous eye, and flecks of serum gathered at the corners of his mouth. She noticed the jumbled wreckage of his teeth. He stopped, and watched her, spreading the silence before her as a salesman would a sample of some wonderful costly stuff. She listened to him holding his breath. There was a wickerwork darn on the heel of his sock. She had a fleeting vision of what his rooms would be, the dust, the worn patch in the carpet, the tired light motionless in the corners. She roused herself.

– Yes, she said, smoothing her apron on her knee. Yes I see.

I sat on the sofa, looking at Mr Pender in silent amaze. His presence was an enormous and somehow daring violation. He smiled nervously when he glanced in my direction, and raised his voice and spoke rapidly, as if to hold something at bay. My mother looked at me as at an exotic, bright-plumed bird that had alighted suddenly in her parlour. First there was Father Barker and his high hopes, and now this. She felt a familiar, angry bafflement. The things he was saying, these plans, these propositions, she did not like them, she was frightened of them. They were incongruous here, like that expensive hat on the table, the cane he was twisting in his chalk-white hands. At last he rose. She showed him to the door.

– So glad, so glad to have met you, Mrs Swan.

She was suddenly tired of him and his precious manner, his smile, his gestures, the way he said her name, pressing it softly upon her like a blandishment. Outside the door he hesitated, eyeing the tender trees in the square. He should try once more, he knew, to impress this dim little woman, to wring a promise from her, but she looked so fearsome, with her arms folded and her mouth set, and he did not relish the prospect of a scene. But oh, did she realize, did she, what an extraordinary – what an amazing – ? Anger and frustration reared up in him like a wave and broke, leaving a wash of sadness in their wake. How do I know these things? I just do. I am omniscient, sometimes. He smiled bleakly and turned away, lifting a finger from the knob of his cane in melancholy farewell.

When he was gone a hectic gaiety flourished briefly, as if the house like a frail vessel had brushed against disaster and survived. Then a thoughtful silence descended.

Uncle Ambrose called. He hesitated inside the door, sniffing at the strained atmosphere. He was a larger version of my father. His body was too big for the small head perched on it. He had close-set eyes and crinkly hair, and a raw, protuberant chin, deeply cleft and mercilessly shaved, like a tiny pair of smarting buttocks. He treated his ugliness with jealous attention, dressing it richly, pampering and petting it, as a mother with a defective child. Still his suits were always a shade too tight, his shoes a little too shiny. Silence came off him in wafts, like an intimation of pain. He seemed always on the point of blurting out some terrible, anguished confession. His reticence, his air of pained preoccupation, lent him a certain authority in our house. His opinion was respected. My mother told him of the teacher's visit, flaring her nostrils and almost shouting, as if she were recounting an insult. *Put him in my hands*, Mr Pender had urged her, smiling his tense, toothed smile. Uncle Ambrose nodded seriously.

– Is that so? he said with care.

She waited. Uncle Ambrose continued to avoid her eye. She turned angrily to the stove, taking down a frying pan from a nail on the wall. My father had risen quietly and was making for the door. *Bang* went the pan. He stopped in the doorway and looked back at her over his glasses. He was in shirt-sleeves and braces, with the weekly paper in one hand and the doorknob in the other. He sighed.

– What? he said dully. What is it?

– Nothing! she cried, without turning, and laughed grimly. Not a thing!

She slapped a string of sausages on the pan, and a whoosh of smoke and flying fat shot up. My father stood breathing. Their squabbles were like that, a glitter in air, over in a flash, like a knife-throwing act.

Jack Kay, dozing by the range, started awake with a grunt. He cast a covert glance about him, licking his lips. He despised old age, its hapless infirmities. He drew himself upright, muttering. He had not liked the sound of Mr Pender at all.

My father returned from the door and sat down heavily, cracking the newspaper like a whip. Uncle Ambrose cleared his throat and considered the carious rim of the sink.

– New people out at Ashburn, he said mildly to no one in particular. Queer crowd.

Uncle Ambrose knew the comings and goings of the town. He drove a hackney motor car, and sat behind the wheel outside the railway station all day waiting for the trains.

My mother would not be diverted. She swept the room with a withering glance and laughed again harshly.

– *Put him in my hands*, indeed! she said.

No one responded. She stood irresolute a moment, flushed and angry, then turned back abruptly to the seething pan. There was another uneasy silence. Uncle Ambrose drummed his fingers on the table, whistling soundlessly. Jack Kay gazed upwards out of a vacant, milky eye, his mouth ajar. My father, moving his lips, scanned the newspaper intently. They seemed ill at ease, trying to suppress something, as if a ghost had walked through their midst and they were pretending they had seen nothing. I looked about at them with interest. Why should they be alarmed? It was at me the spectre had pointed its pale, implacable hand.

IN THE END IT was Mr Pender himself who was spirited away. One day simply he was gone, no one knew where. He had vanished, from school, from his digs, without a trace. Father Barker too was quietly removed. He fell ill, and was sent to the sanatorium. These things came to me like secret signals, indecipherable yet graphic. The summer holidays had begun. I woke in the mornings with a start, as if my name had been called out. The weather, seeming to know something, laid on its loveliest effects. I walked under drowsing trees, through the dreamy silence of sunstruck afternoons, and was so acutely conscious of being there and at the same time almost elsewhere, in a present so fleeting it felt like pure potential, that I seemed to be not so much myself as a vivid memory of someone I had once been. I stood in salt-sharpened sunlight before the glide and glitter of the sea, and the great steady roar of wind in my face was like the future itself bellowing back at me, berating me for being late already.

I spent hours shut away in my room above the square,

hunched over my textbooks, scribbling calculations. Half the time I hardly knew what I was doing, or how I was doing it, or what would come next. Things happened in a flash. One moment the question was there – an equation to be solved, say – the next it was answered, presto! In between, I was aware of only a flicker, a kind of blink, as if a lid had been opened on a blinding immensity and instantly shut again. There might have been someone else inside me doing the calculating, who was surer than I, and infinitely quicker. Indeed, at times this other self seemed about to crack me open and step forth, pristine and pitiless as an imago. Bent there at the table by the bedroom window, I would stop suddenly and lift my head, as if waking in fear out of a muddled dream, my heart thudding dully, while around me in the deepening stillness a sort of presence struggled to materialize. I remembered a picture pinned on the classroom wall when I was a child in the convent school. It was done in satiny pinks and dense, enamelled blues, and showed a laughing little chap playing ball on the brink of a tempestuous river, watched over by a huge figure in white robes, with gold hair and thick gold wings. That was his guardian angel, the nuns said. Every child had a guardian angel. I stared at the picture, struck by the thought of this creature hovering always behind me, with those wings, those wide sleeves, and that look, that to me expressed not solicitude, but a hooded, speculative malevolence.

I had no friends. Figures were my friends. The abacus in my head was never idle. I would devote days to a single exercise, drunk with reckoning. Sometimes at night I woke to discover a string of calculations inching its way through my brain like a blind, burrowing myriapod. A number for me was never just itself, but a bristling mass of other numbers, complex and volatile. I could not hear an amount of money mentioned, or see a date written down, without dismantling the sum into its factors and fractions and roots. I saw mathematical properties everywhere around me. Number, line, angle, point, these were the secret coordinates of the world and everything in it. There was nothing, no matter how minute, that could not be resolved into smaller and still smaller parts.

My mother worried about me. What was I doing up there in that room, all those hours?

– Nothing, I said. Sums.

– Sums? Sums?

She shook her head, bewildered. Behind her, Jack Kay looked at me and smirked.

She nagged me to go out in the fresh air, play games, be a boy like other boys. She would stand motionless on the stairs, as she used to do when I was an infant, and listen to my presence beyond the bedroom door, like a doctor auscultating a suspect heart. I was run down, she said, run down, that was all. She plied me with patented tonics. They tasted of blood and phlegm.

– I'm all right, I would mutter, warding off the brimming spoon. I'm all *right*.

And when she persisted I would get up and walk out, slamming the front door behind me, making the whole house flinch.

I walked and walked. People in the streets passed before me in a blur, like the bars of a cage. When I had exhausted the town I took to the outskirts. I trudged along the Coolmine road, by the rubbish dump, in the sun, my palms wet and my hair hot. There had been a pit-head here in the days when the anthracite was still being worked, the great mine-wheel stood yet, skeletal, motionless and mad. Now the place was a tip for the factories of the town. Lorries from the brick works and the iron foundry would lumber down a rutted track, slewing and whining like crazed ruminants, stop, squat, and drop a pile of rubbish in a fecal rush from their tilted rear ends. Among the dust-hills bands of tinkers scavenged for scrap metal, and old women with sacks slung at their sides grubbed after nuggets of coal, while enormous seagulls settled in flocks, and rose and settled again, furiously crying. Below ground there was a network of tunnels and deep shafts where the mine had been, and now and then suddenly a hole would open in the earth, into which with a sigh a cliff-face of rubble and dust would slowly collapse. It was here that I had my first glimpse of Mr Kasperl. He strolled out of the gateway of the dump one morning with his hands clasped at his back and a cigar in his mouth, a large man with short legs and a big belly. He had an odd, womanly walk, at once ponderous and mincing. He wore a sort of dustcoat that billowed behind him, and black rubber overshoes. The coat, and the galoshes, incongruous on a summer day, were impressive somehow, as if they might have a secret significance, as if they might be insignia denoting some singular, clandestine authority. He had a blunt, cropped head, and little ears, mauve at the tips and delicately whorled, like an exotic variety of fungus. As he passed me by he glanced at me without expression. His eyes were of a washed, impenetrable blue. He went on,

3 3

in the direction of the town, leaving a rich whiff of cigar smoke behind him on the surprised, sunlit air.

Sometimes I went out to Ashburn, and walked where I had walked with my mother years before. Even Miss Kitty was gone now. The big house was padlocked, the park had turned into a wilderness. Here and there, under the dilapidations, signs of a vanished world endured. Pheasants waddled about in the long grass. In the midst of wind-shivered foliage a deer would silently materialize – a glossy eye and a glistening tear-track, a stump of tail, a unicorn's dainty hoof. In a patch of brambles a broken statue leaned at an angle, goggle-eyed and glum, like an inebriated queen. I picked my way through the mute forge, the empty stables, where the air was still hung with the smell of horses. I stood amid the ruins of the cottage where my mother was born. A rapt, intent silence surrounded me, as if everything were watching me, shocked at my intruding in these deserted places. A shell of lupin seeds would pop, or a thrush would whistle piercingly, making me jump. A handful of brick-dust trickling out of a crevice in a crumbling wall seemed a threat hissed at my back.

One day I heard voices. It was noon. A hot wind was blowing. I was standing in an overgrown orchard. No, wait, I was walking along an avenue of beeches, sycamores, something like that. The trees thrashed in the wind, each leaf madly aquiver. The voices wavered, because of the wind I imagine, and at first I could not tell from which direction they were coming, these curiously quaint, minia-ture sounds. Beyond the trees there was a thick high hedge. I came to a gap and squeezed through it, and found myself in a dappled glade that sloped down gently to the edge of a sun-drenched strip of meadow. I stood still, hearing my own breathing, and the wind churning in the trees behind me. My hands were rank with the catpiss smell of privet. Mr Kasperl was walking in the meadow, with a girl at his side. I recognized him at once, there was no mistaking that pigeon-toed gait. Today he wore a shabby white linen jacket and a wide-brimmed straw hat, and was carrying a cane, with which he cuffed the grass idly as he walked. The girl was tall and pale, with long heavy dark hair. Was she clutching a posy of wildflowers? No, no. Her flowered skirt reached to the ground. I noticed the tips of her black pumps, like demure little tongues, peeping out, turn and turn about, at each step, from under the billowing hem, that was damp from the deep grass, and stuck with hayseeds and the dust of buttercups. Mr Kasperl stopped, and lifted his head and looked about him, at the sky, the swaying trees, puffing contemplatively on his cigar, which I could smell even at that distance. The girl went on a little way, but then she stopped too, and stood blankly gazing, her arms hanging at her sides. There was about the two of them a sense of oppression, of stifled restlessness, as if they were captives and this was their daily sip of freedom. I felt an itch of excitement, skulking there in the gloom amid the fleshy odours of leaf and loam. Then nearby something stirred, and my heart plopped on its elastic. Not ten yards from me, leaning against a riven tree, or twined about it, as it seemed at first, was a young man, who must have been there all the time, watching me, while I was watching the others. He was thin, with a narrow foxy face and high cheekbones and a long, tapering jaw. His skin was pale as paper, his hair a vivid red. He wore a shabby pinstriped suit, that had been tailored for someone more robust than he, and a grimy white shirt without a collar. He detached himself from the tree and came forward, examining me with amiable interest.

– What's your name, my man? he said.

– Swan, sir.

He fell back a pace with an extravagant stare, pressing a hand to his breast.

– *Swansir?*

– No, sir. Swan.

– Aha. A cygnet, by Jove.

He took out a dented tin box half filled with cigarette butts, selected one with care, and lit it. He had bad teeth, and a tremor in his hands. He smoked in silence thoughtfully, his head tilted, looking at me with one eye shut.

– My name, he said, is Felix.

He grinned, showing a blackened eye-tooth. The fat man and the girl had advanced across the grass, and stood now below us at the edge of the copse, bending forward a little out of the glare and peering up at us with impassive attention. The girl's long, heart-shaped face was slightly lopsided, as if the left half had slipped a fraction, giving her an expression at once eager and wistful. She was older than I had first thought, a woman, almost. Felix turned to them and called out:

– Swan, he says his name is.

They made no reply, and he looked at me again and winked.

– That, he said, pointing with his thumb, that is Mr Kasperl.

I began to back away. The girl smiled at me suddenly,

and touched the fat man on the shoulder and made a complicated gesture with her hands, but he paid her no heed. Felix, watching me retreat, flicked away his fag-end, and slid his hands into his pockets and grinned.

– Bye bye, bird-boy, he said.

I hurried down the tree-lined avenue, prey to a kind of brimming agitation. I could still see vividly Mr Kasperl's seagull eye, Felix's white, hairless wrists, the girl's sudden smile. Wind roared through the tops of the trees, like something plunging past on its way to wreak havoc elsewhere. I came to the main road, and did not look back. When I got home the house seemed altered, as if some small, familiar thing had been quietly removed.

I next saw Felix and the fat man at Black's Hotel, where my aunt was the manageress. It was morning, and the place had a hangover smell. In the bar the chairs were stacked on the tops of the tables, and a barman in shirt-sleeves stood with his ankles crossed, leaning on the handle of a sweeping-brush. Upstairs somewhere a maid was singing raucously. I padded like a phantom along the hushed corridors. It was like being behind the scenes of some large, frowzy stage production. I spied Mr Kasperl sitting alone by a sunny window in the deserted dining room, drinking coffee, and gazing out at the street with a remote expression. Aunt Philomena was in the cubbyhole she called her office. The air was dense with the reek of face powder and stale cigarette smoke. She was my father's sister, a tall, top-heavy woman, spider-like in her black skirt and black

twinset, with her skinny legs and big behind and bright
demented eyes. I had come to tell her, let me see, to tell her-
oh, what does it matter, I can't think of anything. I wa
about to leave when Felix put his head around the door an
began speaking breezily, calling my aunt by her first name
Seeing me, he stopped. There was silence for a second, an
then he said:

– Well well, who have we here?

Aunt Philomena smiled frantically and blushed, pickin
up things on her desk and putting them down again.

– Oh, this, she said, as though advancing an extenuatin
circumstance, this is my brother's boy.

Felix raised an eyebrow.

– You don't say? he said.

He had recognized me at once, of course.

I walked back along the hushed corridors, past the bar an
the barman, and the dining room with its solitary occupant
and came out by a rear door into dazzling sunlight. A
brewer's dray was backed into the yard, and men in leathe
aprons were heaving barrels into the cellar. Smelling the
bilious stink of beer-suds, I suddenly remembered playing
here one autumn day, years before, with a laughing little
boy in a sailor suit, who was staying with his parents at the
hotel. He had caught a frog, which he kept in a biscuit tin
Watch this, he said to me, and stuck a straw down the frog's
gullet and blew its belly up like a balloon. I remember the
mossy autumnal smell in the yard, the square of blue sky
above us with small, pale-gold clouds. I remember the

boy's elfin face squeezed up with laughter, and his little wet
tongue wedged fatly at the corner of his mouth. I remember
the frog too, the pale distended belly, the twitching legs,
the eyes that seemed about to pop out of their sockets. The
boy kept blowing it up and letting it deflate again. Can that
be possible? It's what I remember, what does it matter
whether it's possible or not. The thing seemed unable to
die. At last it fell on the ground with a wet smack, like a
sodden glove, and squirmed into a corner, trying to get
away. Oh no you don't! the little boy said, and laughed, and
stamped down hard with the heel of his patent-leather shoe.
There was a noise like a loud belch, and something pink
flew up in an arc and splattered on the ground behind me.
Billy, that was the boy's name, I've just remembered it.
Billy, yes. But patent-leather shoes? A sailor suit?

Mr Kasperl came in from Ashburn to the hotel every
morning and sat in the dining room for an hour, drinking
coffee and brooding by the window. People passing by in
the street peered in at him, not inquisitively, but with a
faint, dreamy smile, forgetting themselves. It was as if
something such as he had long been expected, and now it
had arrived at last, and was only a little disappointing.
Sometimes Felix came with him, and prowled about the
hotel with his hands in his pockets, talking to the waitresses
and the kitchen staff and the girls who did the beds. He
made them laugh. He had an actorly way of speaking, in
asides, as it were, as if for the benefit of an invisible
audience. He put on different voices too, it was hard to

know which one was his own. When he told a joke he would laugh and laugh, and go on laughing after everyone else had fallen uneasily silent, as if there were behind the joke something far funnier that only he knew. He was a scream, everyone said so. Only Mr Kasperl seemed impervious to his wit. The fat man would look at him blankly, in silence, and Felix would turn and tiptoe away, doubled up in soundless mirth, a hand clapped over his mouth and his eyebrows waggling.

Aunt Philomena was captivated. Felix and Mr Kasperl were so different from the usual clientele at Black's, the travelling salesmen and the fat-necked cattle-buyers, so coarse, so prosaic. This pair were like something she herself might have invented, for she was given to fantasies, and saw herself always at the centre of some impossible drama. She shared the family home in Queen Street with Uncle Ambrose. When she came to our house now she wore a look of triumph, as if with the arrival of Felix and the fat man all her wild flights had somehow, at last, been vindicated. She told us of Mr Kasperl's little ways, how he liked his coffee strong and boiling hot, and how some days he would stir himself suddenly and call for a glass of brandy, and drink it off in one go, with a brisk snap of the head.

– And that coat! she cried. And the galoshes!

His English was not good, it was hard to understand him. His accent made the things he said seem at once profound and quaint, like ancient pronouncements. He was very educated, he had studied everything, philosophy, science, oh, everything! He had given up all that now, though. Saying this, she put on a tragic face, as if she too had renounced weighty things in her time, and knew all about it. I thought of Mr Kasperl sitting alone by the blazing window in Black's, glooming out at the town like a decrepit god overseeing a world, weary of his own handiwork, but stuck with it.

– What is he doing here, anyway? my mother said. What does he want?

She did not like at all the thought of these people moving into Ashburn, her Ashburn. Aunt Philomena frowned, pursing her vermilion mouth.

– I don't know that he wants anything, she said with dignity. What would he want, here?

No one could answer that. She cast an arch glance about her.

– In fact, she said, he's something to do with mining . . .

Jack Kay snorted.

– Foreigner, is he? he said. Some class of a jewboy, if you ask me.

The subject had provoked in him a mysterious, smouldering rage. Aunt Philomena delicately ignored him.

– An engineer, I believe, she said mildly.

– Engineer, my arse! Jack Kay shouted, and struck his fist on the arm of his rocking-chair.

He glared around him. A dribble of spit had run down his chin. He sucked it up angrily. There was silence. Aunt Philomena cleared her throat and lifted her eyebrows, touching a fingertip to her blue-black perm, to the hem of her skirt, to the mole on her humid upper lip.

– Well! she said softly, expelling a breath, and rose haughtily, like a ship's figurehead, and swept out of the house.

I WENT OUT TO Ashburn day after day, and crouched in the little grove above the sunlit meadow. It was there that the girl found me, as I hoped, no, as I knew she would, came up behind me without a sound one afternoon and put her hand on my shoulder. I turned, I could feel my face grinning madly. She stood very close to me, examining me intently with her eager, lopsided smile, and made a sort of mewling sound at the back of her throat. I felt as if I had come face to face with a creature of the wild, a deer, perhaps, or a large, delicate, fearless bird. I started to say something, but she shook her head, and touched a finger lightly to her ear and lips, to show me she was deaf, and could not speak.

She stepped away from me through the young trees, looking back and gesturing for me to follow. I hesitated, and she nodded vigorously, beckoning and smiling. She wore the same flowered skirt she was wearing the first time I saw her, and a white blouse damp-stained at the armpits. We walked up the meadow. The day was hot, with a listless breeze. Everything seemed to quiver faintly, the air, the grass, the very trunks of the trees, as if all had been struck a huge, soft blow. I glanced at the girl and found her inspecting me avidly, her eyes gleaming and her smiling lips compressed, as if I were something she had caught, and intended to keep. The house, glimpsed through the trees, with the sun in its windows, flashed out at me its impassive signal. We came to a cart track and she took up a stick and scratched her name in the stony clay. Sophie. She pointed to herself, trying to say it, the pale pulp of her tongue lolling between her teeth.

We came to the house, and climbed the steps to the front door. Sophie produced a huge iron key from a pocket of her skirt. In the hall a rhomb of sunlight basked on the floor, like a reclining acrobat. The wallpaper hung down in strips, stirring now in the draught from the doorway like bleached palm-fronds. There was a dry, brownish smell, as of something that had finished rotting and turned to dust. On the threshold a barrier seemed to part before me, an invisible membrane. The air was cool and dry. There was no sign of life. Dust lay everywhere, a mouse-grey, flocculent stuff, like a layer of felt, cushioning our footfalls. We went into a large, darkened room. The shutters were drawn, bristling with slanted blades of sunlight. There was a skitter of tiny claws in a corner, then silence. Sophie opened the shutters. The room greeted the sudden glare with a soundless exclamation of surprise. An armchair leaned back, its armrests braced, in an attitude of startlement and awe. We stood looking about us for a moment, then abruptly Sophie took my hand and drew me after her out of the room and up the wide staircase. She ran ahead of me through the shuttered bedrooms, flinging them open to the radiant day. She laughed excitedly, making gagging noises, her chin up and jaw thrust out as if to prevent something in her mouth from spilling over. I could still feel, like a fragment of secret knowledge, the cool moist print of her hand in mine. I followed her from window to window. The hinged flap of a shutter came away in my grasp like a huge, grey, petrified wing, another collapsed in a soft explosion of rotted wood and paint flakes and the brittle husks of woodworm larvae. Higher and higher we went, the house becoming a stylised outdoors around us, with all that light flooding in, and the high, shadowy ceilings the colour of clouds, and the windows thronging with greenery and sky.

The attic was a warren of little low rooms opening on to each other like an image repeating itself into the depths of a mirror. It was hot and airless up here under the roof. Outside, swifts were shooting like random arrows in and out of the eaves. In what had been a schoolroom I put my hand to a globe of the world, and immediately, as if it had been biding its time, the lacquered ball fell off its stand and rolled across the floor with a tinny clatter. Sophie showed me a narrow room with a sloped ceiling and one circular window, like a wide-open eye. There was a bed, and a bentwood chair, and a washstand with a pitcher and a chipped, enamelled basin. Under a bare lightbulb two flies were lazily weaving the air. This was her room. The window held a view of treetops and far fields. We went along a dim corridor. I glanced through a half-open doorway and saw Mr Kasperl reclining on a vast, disordered bed in his waistcoat and boots, smoking a cigar and studying what appeared to be a large chart or map.

Appeared to be, I like that. He looked at me briefly, without surprise, then turned back to his work.

Sophie led the way downstairs again. Little tremors of excitement still ran through her. Now and then a tiny, high-pitched flute-note, like a restless sleeper's sigh, flew up of its own accord out of her throat. She showed me things she had found about the place, an elaborate doll's house, a dressmaker's dummy on a stand, stark as an exclamation mark, a box of marionettes with tangled strings and splayed limbs, like a heap of miniature hanged men. She crawled on hands and knees into a closet under the stairs and dragged out a trunk of mouldering fancy-dress costumes. She watched me eagerly, with intensity, her eyes fixed on my face, my lips. Then she frowned, and pushed away the marionettes and shut the lid of the trunk, and sat back on her heels and sighed, as if these things, these dolls and dresses and bits of silk, were things she was telling me, and I was not responding. In a moment, though, she was up again and running down the hall, beckoning me to follow. She opened a heavy, studded door on to a little room rigged up as a photographic studio. The place was cluttered with parts of antique cameras and foxed packets of chemicals and stacks of glass negatives. The light was dense and still. Sophie sat down on a bench with a bundle of dog-eared, grainy prints in her lap. She patted the place beside her, inviting me to sit. There was a faint, feverish hum in the hot air, and a sharp, chemical tang. Gravely I examined the pictures as she passed them to me one by one. She had been through them before, she had her favourites, a close-up of a stout baby with the head of a blank-eyed caesar, a crooked shot of a donkey wearing a straw hat, a formal portrait of

servants arrayed like an orchestra on the front steps of th
house on some long-ago summer afternoon. Towards th
bottom of the pile the subjects changed. Here was a bac
view of a large lady in a bustle leaning over a balcony, whi
behind her a whiskered gentleman gazed in lively surmise
a plump, cleft peach he was holding in his hand and about
bite. There were studies of the same couple, he in droopi
leotard now and she stripped to her corset, posing on
ornate bed in postures at once lewd and oddly decorou
There was something sad about them, these jet a
pearl-grey ghosts, whose future was already our past. T
final picture was of the woman alone. She sat naked astri
a straight-backed chair, grinning into the camera, with h
hands on her bulging hips and her legs thrust wide apa
Her sex, defenceless and thrilling, was like some intrica
tasselled creature brought up from the secret depths of t
sea. I cleared my throat and looked sideways at Sophie. S
was watching me again, with that intent, expectant smi
There were violet shadows under her eyes, and a faint, da
down on her upper lip. She had a milky odour, wi
something sharp in it, like the smell of crushed nettles. H
hair was a hot, heavy mass, I could sense it, the dark weig
of it, the thickness. She put aside the pictures, and we le
the studio and wandered into a large, long room wi
glass-fronted bookcases lining the walls and plaster moul
ings on the ceiling. The bookcases were empty. Fren
windows gave on to the glare of the sweltering day, makin
the room seem a vast, dim tent. There had been intrud
here, there was a broken window-pane, and dead leaves
the carpet, and in the corner on the floor a huge, rusted tu
I opened wide the windows and stood looking out. Sto

4 6

steps led down to a sunken garden with waist-high grass. The air throbbed, big with heat. A little brown bird flitted up into a tree without a sound. Sophie put a record on an ancient gramophone and cranked the handle. There was a splutter and a hiss, and a wobbly orchestra struck up a waltz. The music swayed out on the summer air, quaint and gay. She knelt in a sagging armchair, with her hands folded along the back of it and her chin on her hands, watching the disc go round and round. I wondered if she could feel the music, a kind of drunken buzzing in her head, as of someone a long way off playing on paper and comb. The waltz tottered to a close, and she took off the record and put it back carefully in its sleeve. I can see it still, that scene, the shiny arm of the gramophone, curved and fat like the arm of a baby, and the chrome nipple twinkling at the centre of the turntable, and Sophie's slender hands lifting the record. What else? The way the turntable continued spinning silently, with comic, breakneck haste, like a dog chasing its tail. What else? The burgundy-red label of the record. The picture on the label of the little dog chasing its tail, no, listening, with one ear cocked. What else? The brown-paper sleeve, with one corner turned down. What else? What else?

Felix was sitting in the kitchen, sorting through a collection of old keys of all shapes and sizes spread before him on the table. The room was narrow, with a high ceiling and low windows, their sills level with an unruly patch of lawn outside. There was a chipped sink, and an angry-looking, soot-black stove. The sink was stacked with soiled crockery, and something was bubbling sluggishly in a battered pot on the stove. Felix looked at me and grinned.

– Well, he said, if it isn't Sweetsir Swansir. Can't keep away from us, eh?

Sophie peered into the steaming stewpot and wrinkled her nose. She brought plates and mugs and set them out on the table, shoving Felix's keys unceremoniously to one side. He leaned back with a lazy sigh, studying me idly, one arm hitched over the back of his chair and his thin mouth stretched in a smile. I heard a step behind me. Mr Kasperl had appeared in the doorway.

– And the dead arose and appeared to many! Felix murmured.

The fat man sat down at the table, lowering his bulk heavily on to the chair, which cried out in protest under him. He gouged a knuckle into his eyes, then sat gazing blearily at his plate.

– Had a little rest, did we? Felix shouted playfully, wagging his head at him across the table. Had a little kip?

Sophie brought the saucepan from the stove and ladled a smoking dollop of dark-brown stew on to each plate. Felix waved an arm expansively, inviting me to join them. I sat down opposite Mr Kasperl.

Sophie poured out tea from a blackened pot. There was a little nest of cobwebs in the bottom of my mug. Mr Kasperl coughed moistly one, twice, and then a third time, inclining an ear, as if testing something inside him. The heat hummed, pressing on the house. Birds were singing weakly outside. The high, narrow room teetered above us, as if we were at the bottom of a deep shaft. A scalded spider bobbed to the surface of my tea, turning in slow circles. I felt Mr Kasperl's gaze directed at me. We looked at each other for a moment. I fancied I could see something stirring, like torpid fish, in the dead depths of his eyes. He stopped chewing suddenly, and, puckering his lips, extracted a piece of gristle from his mouth and set it down with deliberation on the side of his plate. I looked away. Sophie was watching me, and so was Felix. They were all three watching me, with calm and somehow remote attention, as if they had turned to look back at me from the far side of a valley, waiting to see if I would come across and join them.

I MET FELIX IN town one day. He came ambling along Owl Street with his hands in his pockets, whistling. I felt a spasm of that same excitement, a sort of eager fright, that I had felt the first time I saw him, in the grove above the meadow. I thought of turning aside, but he had already seen me. The street was narrow and steep, running athwart a hill above the harbour. The spire of the Church of the Assumption beetled over the rooftops, seeming somehow in flight. There was a smell of sea-wrack, and a gamy stench from a poulterer's yard up a lane.

– Hello, whooper, he said. Going my way?

– No, I said, I . . .

– Oh well, I'll go yours, then.

He grinned.

We walked down the hill towards the harbour. Sunlight lay along one side of the street, wedged at the foot of a deep diagonal of shadow. Few people were about. An old man in rags was crossing the road on a crutch. At each laborious step he brought his left foot down on the asphalt with an angry bang. He stopped in the gutter and waited intently, panting, as we went past. From this high place we could look out over the town, a huddle of dark geometry spread before us in the summer haze. Felix paused, and took a cigarette butt from his box and fingered it thoughtfully, picking charred crumbs of tobacco from the blackened tip.

– I've been talking to your auntie, he said. She says you're a wizard with figures.

He struck a match and held the flame suspended, and glanced at me sideways.

– That right? he said.

Out in the harbour a marker bell was ringing and ringing. I could feel the blood flooding into my face. I walked on quickly, and Felix followed. Behind me the cripple banged his hoof, and, unless I imagine it, laughed.

We turned into Goat Alley. Already Felix knew his way about these back streets. He steered me across a sunny yard behind a fishmonger's shop and down a narrow flight of slimed stone steps. A rat scuttled ahead of us, dragging a fish-head in its teeth. We came abruptly on to the quayside. The sea was high, swaying sluggishly beyond the wood-works like the smooth pale humped back of something living. A bronze pikeman, sombrely agleam in the sun-light, pointed a rope-veined forearm in the direction of the railway station. We crossed to the woodworks. Beneath us we could hear the tide's vague slap and slither. Felix threw his fag-end into the water, it made a tiny hiss. In the harsh sea-light the whites of his eyes were soiled, and the skin around his eyes was taut, as if from a scorching, and scored with tiny wrinkles like cracks in a china glaze. The breeze brought me a waft of his breath, laden with the smell of smoke and the metallic tang of his bad teeth. I could smell his clothes too, with the sun on them, the shiny, pinstriped jacket with its prolapsed pockets and wilting lapels, the concertina trousers, the shoes like boats.

– Mr Kasperl was asking about you, he said. Wanted to know who you were. I told him. I said, he's a prodigy, that boy. He was interested.

– Why, I said, why was he asking about me?

– Eh? Oh, I don't know. The subject came up. Listen, here's a good one. How does a lady hold her liquor? By the ears. Ha!

We walked on. Our footsteps thudded on the tarred boards, the sea sucked and slapped. Felix talked and talked. He put on his funny voices, did impressions, recounted queer stories. He talked about the war, about the Germans and the Japs, and the sulphur bombs that were dropped on Dresden. He knew all the facts, the figures. He stopped suddenly and struck a pose, with one hand on his heart and the other pointing heavenward, and gaily sang:

> Oh, the Jews nailed Jesus,
> But Jesus screwed the Jews!

He speculated about the last secret of Fatima, which is so terrible the Pope keeps it sealed in a vault in the Vatican. Maybe, he said, maybe it had something to do with the three dark days that will herald the end of the world, when nothing will light except blessed candles made of beeswax. He clapped his hands and cackled.

– Get that candle out! he cried. As the Mother Superior said to the nun.

We left the quay and walked up through the town. The main street was busy. Felix smiled on everything, as if all this, the streets, the people, the shop windows decked with corsets and carpenter's tools, had been laid on specially for his amusement. The housewives doing their shopping eyed us with interest. They all knew Felix. He greeted them genially, waving and bowing, doffing an imaginary tricorn, and all the while making disparaging remarks to me about them out of the side of his mouth. We passed by the malt store, and the place where the Horse River ran under the road, and so came to our square. We stopped under the trees, by the horse trough, a metal tub surmounted by an iron swan painted white, that spouted a weak jet of water through a rusted beak.

– Swan, Felix said, pointing. Ha ha.

This was where, years ago, the dwarf used to sit on his tricycle and talk to me, smoothing a hand on his oiled hair and shooting his immaculate cuffs. Felix lounged against the trough, his arms and ankles crossed. Suddenly I wanted to tell him something, anything, to confide in him, the urge was so strong that for a second tears prickled under my eyelids and my throat grew thick. He was watching me with a little smile, his eyes narrowed against the light.

– I'd say we're a lot alike, you know, he said, you and me.

A flock of starlings rose from the trees and flew over our heads in a rush of wings, briefly darkening the air. My mother came to the front door of our house and stood with her sleeves rolled, watching us. Felix met her baleful stare with a mockingly apologetic smile. I turned my back on her. She went inside again, and slammed the door. Felix stretched himself, yawning. He considered the sky, the rooftops, the delicate green of the trees.

– But seriously, he said, figures, now, that's very interesting. Mr Kasperl is very interested, really.

When I went into the house my mother said nothing. I went up to my room. My books, papers, pencils, were on the table, by the window. They wore somehow a knowing air.

I began to go out regularly then to Ashburn. My presence was accepted without remark, I might have been part of the household. Felix and I played cards at the kitchen table, and ate Sophie's stews. I walked with her in the grounds, or explored the house with her. Mr Kasperl paid me no heed at all, except that sometimes when we came face to face unexpectedly he would give me one of his remote, dull stares and frown vaguely, as if he thought he might vaguely know me.

My mother wanted to know where I was spending my time now. She had preferred it when I shut myself away in my room, that silence above her head had been less alarming than these inscrutable absences. But at home these days I felt like an exile come back on a brief, bored visit. How small it all seemed, how circumscribed. At Ashburn the horizon was limitless. I moved in a new medium there, a dense, silvery stuff that flashed and shimmered, not like air at all, but a pure fluid that held things fixed and trembling, like water in the brimming jet of a fountain.

I brooded on Sophie as one of Mr Pender's more difficult

puzzles. She would not solve. There was a flaw in her, a tiny imbalance, that would not let the equation come out, it showed in the slope of her shoulders, in her delicate, long, lopsided face. Her walk was a swift, strong swimming in air. She favoured her left side, so that at every step she seemed about to veer away impetuously to the right, as if there were things out there clamouring softly for her attention. She was always moving, always ahead of me, I knew intimately the shell-like hollows behind her ankle-bones, the fissured porcelain at the backs of her knees, the syncopated slow wingbeat of her shoulder-blades. She seemed built not on bone but on some more supple framework. Her thumbs were double-jointed. She could pick up things with her toes. She was given to rushes of playful violence, she would turn on me suddenly with a gagging laugh and give me a push, or hit me hard on the shoulder with her sharp little fist. She had a way of stiffening suddenly with a gasp and clasping herself in her arms, as if to keep herself from exploding. Even at her stillest she gave off ripples of excitement, like a huntress poised behind a pillar with bent bow. She was a sealed vessel, precarious, volatile, filled to bursting with all there was to say. She might have been not mute but merely waiting, holding her breath. Her deafness was like vigilance. She would fix on the most trivial thing with rapt attention, as if anything, at any moment, might begin to speak to her, in a small voice, out of that huge, waveless sea of silence in which she was suspended. She communicated in an airy, insubstantial language consisting not of words but moving forms, transparent, yet precise and sharp, like glass shapes in air. When I was away from her I could not

5 5

think how exactly she managed it. She seldom resorted to the sign alphabet, and then impatiently, making a wry face, as if she had been forced to shout. However, these quick, deft displays never failed to surprise and impress me. They seemed a sort of sleight of hand, adroit and faintly jubilant. Mr Kasperl, though he appeared to understand what she was saying, would make little response, but stand before her with his head lowered, looking at her blankly from under his brow, his mysterious thoughts elsewhere. Felix just laughed at her, waving his arms to fend her off, as if she were making preposterous demands of him.

– Listen to her! he would say to me merrily. She's mad, mad!

And she too would laugh, and mime exasperation, shaking a playful fist in his face.

Felix was always busy, in a vague, haphazard way. He never seemed to finish anything, or to have started anywhere, but was always just doing. The keys he had been sorting the first time I came to the house lay for weeks on the kitchen table. He would walk up and stand looking at them, his hands in his pockets and his chin sunk on his breast, and heave a histrionic, weary sigh before wandering off to tackle some other obscure task. He spent hours prowling about upstairs, rummaging in closets and under beds, or going through the wardrobes that stood, like broad sarcophagi, in dank dressing rooms and faded boudoirs, still thronged with clothes, the moth-eaten relics of generations of Ashburns. He would salvage odds and ends of antique outfits – a pair of check plus-fours, a mildewed dinner jacket, a cricket umpire's floppy hat – and wear them around the house with bland aplomb. I came upon him one day in the grounds, strolling through the trees in baggy tweeds and a norfolk jacket and carrying a rusty shotgun.

– Thought I'd take a bang at the birds, don't you know, he said. Care to be my loader?

It had been raining, and now a sharp sun was shining. The drenched woods glittered. We walked along a winding path. There were rustlings and slitherings all about us in the grass, under the leaves. I had not rid myself of a faint unease in his presence. I always answered his remarks too eagerly, smiled too quickly at his jokes, as if to hold him at arm's length. He made fun of everything. He pulled faces at Mr Kasperl behind his back, imitating his matronly walk. He would throw back his head and feign loud laughter, as if someone had said something wonderfully funny, until Sophie, with the inept cunning of the deaf, began to laugh along with him, then he would put up a hand and hide his face from her and chuckle, winking at Mr Kasperl and me. Yet it was not his mockery I feared. We came to a viridian field. The verdure shimmered. A little band of grazing deer saw us and fled silently into a copse. We paused, and Felix looked about him, beaming.

– What a paradise it seems, all the same, he said. I sometimes wonder if we deserve this world. What do you think, bird-boy?

He laughed and sauntered on, hefting the shotgun in the crook of his arm. We walked along the margin of the field until we came to the high hedge and the drive. The house was handsome with the sun on it, the windows ablaze. Birds swooped through the rinsed air, the great trees stood as if listening. For a moment I experienced a pure, piercing happiness, unaccountable, fleeting, like a fall of light. A delivery boy was coming up the drive behind us on his bike, pedalling leisurely, with one hand on the handlebar and his knees splayed. I knew him. His name was Clancy, a short, muscular fellow with a swatch of coarse black hair and a crooked jaw, and a bad cast in one eye. He wore big boots with cleats, and a long, striped apron. He had been in my class at school years ago. He was a dunce, and sat at a desk by himself in a corner. The teachers made fun of him, holding up his copybooks for us to see his slovenly work, while he crouched in his seat and looked around at us murderously out of his crooked eye. Sometimes on these occasions he would break down and weep, shockingly, like an adult, in pain and rage, coughing up jagged sobs and clenching his inky fists helplessly in his lap. Now, spying me ahead of him, he stopped whistling abruptly, and the front wheel of his bicycle wobbled. Felix halted, and waited, watching him. He dismounted and crossed to the other side of the drive, and plodded along slowly, bent low and pushing the bike, frowning to himself as if a very important thought had just occurred to him. The bicycle was a sturdy black machine with small thick wheels, and at the front an enormous wicker basket filled with parcels.

– You there, Felix called imperiously. Who are you?

Clancy stopped, and peered about him with an elaborate air of startlement. He used to wait for me on the way home from school and knock me down and pummel me, sitting on my chest and breathing his feral breath in my face. His fury always seemed a sort of grief. In time a hot, awful intimacy had grown up between us. Now, stricken with embarrassment, we avoided each other's eye, as if we had once committed sin together. He opened his mouth, shut it, then coughed and tried again. He was eyeing the gun cradled in Felix's arm.

– From Walker's, sir, he said thickly. With the messages.

– Messages? Felix said. What messages?

Clancy began to sweat. He licked his lips, and pointed to the parcels in the basket.

– Them, sir. The messages that was ordered.

Felix turned to me.

– What is the fellow talking about? he said. Have you any idea?

– The grocery messages, Clancy said, raising his voice. The ones that was . . .

– Oh, *groceries*, Felix said, with a little laugh. I see, yes. Well, have you the list, then?

– What, sir?

Felix looked to heaven and sighed.

– The list, *sor*! The list that was given to the shop. Have you it with you?

Clancy blinked slowly and wiped his nose on a knuckle.

– I'd say I have, all right, he said guardedly.

He leaned his bicycle on its stand and produced a fistful of grubby papers from the pocket of his apron, and began to leaf through them unhappily with a thick thumb.

– Well, read it out, man, Felix cried, read it out!

A dark flush appeared on Clancy's pitted brow. He licked his lips again and bent over his bits of paper, scrutinizing them with a stolid, hopeless stare. Felix groaned in annoyance.

– Come on, man! he said. What's wrong with you?

Clancy, his face on fire, looked at me at last, like a wounded animal, in fury and a sort of supplication. He was not able to read. A moment passed. I looked away from those beseeching eyes. Felix chuckled.

– Oh, go on then, he said to Clancy, take your stuff around to the back door.

Clancy thrust the papers into his pocket, and mounted his bike and pushed off towards the house, crouched over the handlebars as if battling against a gale. Felix grinned, shaking his head. Suddenly he tossed the shotgun to me. The weight of it was a surprise.

– Go ahead, Barabbas, he said. Blaze away.

W O R K M E N B E G A N arriving at the house, singly, with a fist in a pocket and one arm tightly swinging, or shouldering along in silent groups of two or three. Sophie and I watched them from the upstairs windows. They grew steadily foreshortened as they approached, as if they were wading into the ground. They would knock once at the front door and step back, holding their caps in their hands, quite patient, waiting. They wore shapeless jackets and white shirts open at the neck, and trousers larded with grime. Their faces and the backs of their necks glowed, I pictured them bent over sinks in cramped sculleries at first light, scrubbing themselves raw. One had a bald patch, pink and neat as a tonsure. They were roadmen and casual labourers, and a few factory hands laid off from the brick works or the foundry. Mr Kasperl interviewed them in one of the big empty rooms downstairs. He sat at a battered, leather-topped desk before the window, fiddling with a stub of pencil, while Felix walked up and down and did the talking. The men, standing in a knot in the middle of the floor, avoided looking at each other, as if out of a sort of shame. They pretended unconcern, hitching up their belts and glancing around them at the damp-stained walls and the crumbling cornices. Felix harangued them jovially, like a fairground barker.

– All right, now, all right, he said, show us your muscles there. We only want good strong types, willing to work. That right, boss?

Mr Kasperl looked at him silently, twiddling the pencil in his heavy hands. The men grinned and mumbled, shuffling their feet.

In the end they all got hired, even the one with the bald spot. One morning I arrived and found them gathered in front of the house, with shovels over their shoulders, smoking cigarettes and muttering among themselves. A lorry with its engine going stood on the drive, a clumsy, upright model with a sort of chimney sticking up, and no mudguards. It shuddered like a sick horse, belching up black spurts of exhaust smoke. The tailgate was crusted with traces of dung, the mark of a previous life. Felix got down from behind the wheel and herded the workers aboard. He winked at me, and mimed exhaustion, drooping his shoulders and letting his jaw hang sideways. Mr Kasperl, in dustcoat and overshoes, paused in front of the house and looked about him at the bright morning with a grim, disparaging eye, then descended the steps with his mincing tread and hauled himself, grunting, into the cab. Felix ground the gears and swung the wheel, and the lorry moved off falteringly in a cloud of dust and diesel fumes. One of the workmen standing in the back gave a half-hearted whoop, and then grinned sheepishly and stared hard ahead. The noise of the engine died away in the direction of Coolmine, and the heedless song of a thrush, that had been there all the time, welled up in the stillness.

There was a sense of airy emptiness in the house. I climbed the stairs as if ascending a rope into the blue. Sophie was above me on the landing, looking down at me, hands braced on the rail, her face suspended in a vault of air, like a trapeze artist poised to leap. We wandered through the attic. The floors were tense as trampolines under our feet. I thought of all those rooms below us with no one in them, the sky going about its enormous, stealthy business in the windows, the sun inching its complex geometry across the dusty floors.

In Sophie's room we sat down on the bed. I had tried to teach her something about numbers here, showed her match games, and tricks with algebra, laying out my gift before her on the quilt. I had entertained high hopes. How could she resist these things, their simplicity and elegance, the way move by move the patterns grew, like crystals assembling in clear, cold air? But it was no good, she looked at the numbers and at me, her eyes empty, her face a smiling mask. Her silence was a kind of absence. And so I gave up. Now she raised herself on one knee, stretching to peer out the round window above us. She had brought up the box of marionettes and was repairing them, they were strewn on the floor among paintpots and brushes and jars of glue. She tapped me on the shoulder, wanting me to look at something down on the drive. When I made to rise she lost her balance for a moment, and fell against me in a flurry of hands and breath and tumbling hair. Her skin was cool, I could feel the heat of my own suddenly flushed face reflected back at me from her smooth brow and shadowed cheeks. She drew away from me with a little, gurgling laugh. She had kissed me, or I had kissed her, I don't know, so lightly, so fleetingly, I thought at first I had imagined it. My heart wobbled, like something swaying on an edge and about to fall. She had raised herself to the window again and was looking out. She turned and smiled, not at me this time, but in the direction of the doorway. Felix was there, regarding us with a glint of amusement.

– Please, don't get up, he said slyly. It's only me.

He ambled into the room, casting a sideways glance at the marionettes on the floor. I had not heard the lorry returning. His boots had black mud on them, and there were faint black streaks, like traces of war-paint, on his forehead and his jaw. He said:

– Hell down pit, lad.

Sophie was motioning him excitedly to the window. He came and stood behind her, craning to see where she was pointing. Below, on the gravel in front of the house, Jack Kay was standing, hatted, in Sunday suit, leaning on his malacca stick. He was looking up, I wondered if he could see us, our three heads crowded in the staring window high above him. Felix turned his face to me, a grinning indian.

– Who's that, now, I wonder? he said. Looks familiar, I think.

Jack Kay was climbing the steps, then we heard his distant knock at the front door. Felix put a finger to his lips. He sat down on the bed, and Sophie knelt behind him, leaning eagerly over his shoulder. He reached into a pocket of his jacket, then turned up his hand to her and opened it slowly. A tiny brown mouse crouched in his palm, its whiskers and the pink tip of its nose aquiver. It turned this way and that, sniffing the air with little jerks of its head. Sophie, delighted, tried to take the creature in her hand, but Felix held it teasingly out of her reach, until she made a lunge and captured it. She lifted it level with her face, and mouse and girl studied each other. Then she leaned forward quickly and touched her pursed lips lightly to the quivering snout. Felix laughed.

– Oho! he cried, look, beauty and the beast!

Jack Kay was hammering at the front door down there. Felix heaved a sigh.

– All right, all right! he muttered.

He went out, and presently I heard him below on the steps with Jack Kay. The old man's voice was raised. Sophie sat on her heels on the bed, with the mouse in her lap, stroking it rhythmically with her fingertip, from head to tail, pressing a groove into the fine fur. At each gently dragging stroke the pink cleft at the tip of the creature's sharp little snout opened a fraction and closed again wetly. Sophie bowed her head, her dark hair falling about her face. Her fingernail, gliding amid the parted fur, gleamed like an oiled bead. The room was still. Jack Kay was shouting. The front door slammed. Sophie looked up at me with an intent, attenuated smile, as if she were vaguely in distress. The mouse lay meekly in her lap, minutely throbbing. I took a step forward, it seemed a kind of lurching fall, and reached out a hand to touch the tiny creature. Immediately it sprang from her lap and scurried down the side of the bed. Felix, coming into the room again, said lightly:

– Ah, you haven't the knack. We'll have to teach you, won't we?

He bent down by the bed and coaxed the mouse back on to his palm. He wandered with it to the window and peered out.

– There he goes, he said. Fierce old boy, I must say. He was looking for you, you know, cob. Told him we'd never heard of you. *No Swan here, my man*, I said, *our swans are all geese*. Did I do right?

He looked from me to Sophie and back again. There was silence. I could hear faintly the sound of Jack Kay's boots crunching away over the gravel. Sophie rose from the bed, brushing at her skirt. She glanced at me vaguely, as if she could not quite remember who I was. Felix offered her the mouse, but she walked past him like a sleepwalker, out of the room. He watched her go, then turned his sly glance on me.

– All these my creatures, he whispered gaily, making his eyeballs roll.

He opened his hand and showed me the mouse, lying motionless on its side, its front paws folded, a bubble of ruby blood in its snout.

At home I found Jack Kay sitting sideways at the kitchen table, ashen with rage, one fist planted among the tea-things and the other clamped on the crook of his stick. For the second time in his life he had been put out of Ashburn Park. Who did they think they were, that fat foreigner and that other, red-headed bastard? What right did they have? He glared about him, knuckles whitening, daring anyone to answer. Felix had laughed at him – laughed, at him, Jack Kay!

– God blast him for a whore's melt, he muttered thickly, and dealt the floor a crack with his cane.

He fixed me with a blood-filled eye and grunted, scowling. My mother was silent. It was she, of course, who had sent him out to Ashburn. Now she wore a chastened, thoughtful air. She brought my tea to the table and stood over me, incensed, and yet unnerved. She had felt today the touch of something cold and cruel, a kind of malignancy, as if an illness had taken hold in her. She too had twice lost Ashburn, once as a girl when she left home, and then a second time with the advent of Mr Kasperl and his familiar. Now they were trying to take me from her too. But she would not let them – no, she would not let them! Her hand shook, the cup and saucer rattled, she set them down hurriedly, with a little crash.

I RELIVED THAT moment on Sophie's bed so often in my mind that the details wore out, became hollow, leached of solidity. I alone was always real there, always intensely present. Suddenly I had a vivid sense of myself. I held myself poised, balanced in air, as if I were some precious, polished thing that had been put with ceremonial care into my hands. It was not the kiss that mattered so much, but what it seemed to signify. A world had opened up before me, disordered, perilous and strange, and for the first time in my life I felt almost at home.

But when I next saw Sophie I experienced a tiny jolt of surprise. She had so throbbed in my imagination that now, when I confronted the real she, it was as if I had just parted from her more dazzling double. She must have caught a flicker of that shock in my eyes, for she smiled strangely, and turned and walked away slowly, looking back at me over her shoulder. That was the day she took me to Mr Kasperl's room.

I did not notice her taking me there. We were just trailing aimlessly about the house, as we so often did. But when she pushed open his door I remember feeling a vague, almost pleasurable qualm, as if I were being seduced, gently, with sly blandishments, into hazard. He was not there, he was at the mine. The room was vast, high-ceilinged, crowded with big ugly pieces of furniture, bureaux, a chest of drawers, his enormous, rumpled bed. There was a hushed, watchful atmosphere, as if something had been going on, and had stopped when we came in. It was raining outside, a summer storm was on the way. Sophie wandered to the streaming window and stood with her forehead against the glass, looking out dreamily into a green, liquid world. I glanced at Mr Kasperl's papers strewn on the bed, his books, his ordnance maps, his charts of the underground workings at Coolmine. There was a big black notebook, thick as a wizard's codex, with a worn cloth cover and dog-eared pages. I picked it up idly and opened it, and at once it began to speak to me in a strong, clear, familiar voice. I sat down slowly on the edge of the bed.

It was the work of years. Page after page was crammed with calculations, diagrams, algebraic formulas, set out in a minute, square script. Much of it I could not understand. Quaternions, matrix theory, transfinite numbering, I had barely heard of such things. I noticed there were things we had in common, however, a particular fondness for symmetries, for example, for mirror equivalences, and palindromic series. But his was a grandmaster game, and I was a novice. Such intricacy, such elegance! I read on, enraptured. Everything beyond the bed became blurred, as if a kind of luminous dusk had fallen. The girl seemed to flit about the room, there one moment, gone the next, like a vague attendant seen from a sick-bed. For a while she was standing beside me, her hip negligently touching my shoulder, but when she went away it was as if I had imagined it, that warmth, her shadow, her hand resting at her side. The storm arrived, peals of thunder rolled across the sky, rattling the window-frames. The air had a sulphurous glow. Then suddenly it was calm again, and I looked up in undulant rain-light and found Mr Kasperl standing in the doorway, in his drenched dustcoat, watching me.

He entered the room heavily, mopping the rain on his brow with a large red kerchief. He took off his coat, and, without looking at her, handed it to Sophie. The rain stopped, and the sun came out suddenly, with an almost audible swish, blazing in the window. I closed the notebook quietly and laid it back on the bed. Mr Kasperl paid me no heed, yet his manner was not un-friendly. Sophie fetched a hanger for his coat, and hung it in the window to dry in the sun. He moved here and there about the room, with that slow, deliberate walk, rolling on the balls of his feet. He opened a box of cigars that stood on top of a bureau, selected one, sniffed it, trimmed the end, and lit up. I thought of sidling away quietly. He worked at his cigar unhurriedly, getting it going evenly, then turned at last and came towards the bed. I stood up. He stopped, not looking at me still, and drew a bead on the black notebook, one eye half shut, as if it were a distant target, then picked it up and riffled through the pages. He found what he was looking for, and turned to me, tapping a finger on the page. It was a series of field equations, elegant but enigmatic, their solutions all dissipating towards infinity. He contemplated them for a moment with what seemed a grim satisfaction, then put the open notebook into my hands and walked away from me, leaving cigar smoke, and a faint smell of damp cloth and coal. I sat down on the bed again. The door opened and Felix put in his head. He looked at me with his thin smile, narrowing his eyes.

– I was looking for you, he said, and here you were in the temple, all the time.

He followed his head into the room, one hand in a pocket, scratching his groin. Mr Kasperl padded past him and went out, his silent back stooping through the doorway. Sophie turned to the window again. I put the notebook away.

Jack Kay fell ill. He sat at the range in his rocking-chair, a plaid rug about his knees. He was cold, he said, cold, glaring resentfully at the sunshine streaming in the kitchen window. His large white hands lay motionless in his lap, like a pair of clumsy implements fallen from his grasp. He would not eat. Amber puddles began to appear on the floor under his chair. The doctor was called, and ordered him to bed. We lifted him from the rocker, my father, Uncle Ambrose and I, and carried him upstairs. He lay against us stiffly, a big chalk statue, mute and furious. He was unexpectedly light. The years had been working away at him in secret, hollowing him out. We propped him in bed against a bank of pillows and stepped back, brushing our hands. He gazed up at us fearfully, like a child, his mouth working, his fingers clamped on the fold of blankets at his chest as if it were the rim of a parapet behind which he was slowly, helplessly falling. Days, the doctor said, a week at the most. But the weeks went past and still he lay there, watching the light in the window, the surreptitious sky. He would talk to no one, but raged in silence, like a man betrayed. He developed bedsores, I had to turn him on his side while my mother basted him with ointment. His skin was dry but supple, like wrapping paper with something soft inside it, and I thought of those soft parcels my mother would have me carry home for her from the butcher's when I was a child. In the narrow bed he looked huge yet insubstantial, a great bleached dead husk, inside of which the living man still cowered, peering out through the eyes in panic and a kind of amazement. Summer was ending, but still the weather held, as if to mock him. His mind began to wander. He would lie for hours talking to himself in a furious undertone. Sometimes he shouted out suddenly, and threw himself from side to side, plucking at the bedclothes, like a footless drunkard trying to get up and fight. One day he fell out of bed, we found him on the floor in a tangle of sheets, waving his arms weakly as if to ward off an assailant. His pot was overturned.

– Oh, look what you've done, my mother said. Just look!

He glared at her, suspicious, bewildered, afraid.

– Mother, he said gruffly, are you there, mother?

He groaned. There was no way out of the huge confusion

into which he had blundered. He let us lift him into bed, and lay back on the pillows meekly. He turned his eyes to the window, and one fat, lugubrious tear ran down his temple, over the livid vein pulsing there.

At the funeral my mother could not cry. She watched with melancholy interest as the coffin was lowered into the hole. My father stood to one side fingering his tie. The violet shadow of a cloud swept a far-off meadow. At the edge of the small circle of mourners a figure had appeared, half hidden among a cluster of headstones, his hands in his pockets, a lick of foxy hair plastered on his narrow brow. He smiled at me and winked, and made a little sign, raising three fingers and sketching a sort of rapid blessing. Behind him a stained seraph towered on widespread marble wings.

QUEER THE LANDSCAPES that memory, that old master, chooses for its backgrounds, the twilit distances with meandering rivers and mossy brown crags, and tiny figures in costume doing something inexplicable a long way off. When I think now of that autumn, in a flash I see the malt store, I don't know why. It was a grey stone fortress with a slate roof, and a row of small, barred windows high up under the eaves. Through an opening over the arched entranceway a block and tackle stuck out, like the arm of a complicated gibbet. The malt was dried there before being sent to the breweries. Insinuations of steam escaped at the windows day and night, and the sour, beery stink of the simmering grain pervaded the air. My father's job must have taken him there often, though I never saw him – indeed, now that I think of it, I never saw anyone at all there. Where it stood was known as the Folly, a windswept angle between the backs of two mean streets. The place wore an air of dejection, and a sort of weary knowing. It seems always an overcast and cold October there. Dry leaves like the hands of dead pianists skitter along the pavements with a scraping noise. The wind soughs in the trees, and panels of pale, lumpy cloud pour in silence down a tilted rectangle of sky. A dog is barking in the distance, something is monotonously creaking, and I halt and stand expectantly, as if everything might be about to gather itself together and address me.

School was grotesque now, an absurd and shameful predicament. I had outgrown all this, the noise, the smells, the tedium. Every afternoon when the bell went I set off at once for Ashburn. At Coolmine the gate had been mended, and a warning sign had been put up, with a skull-and-crossbones stencilled on it. From the road I could see the workmen over at the pit-head, toiling like ants. Sometimes I spotted Mr Kasperl too, pacing up and down, or with Felix poring over charts spread out on the bonnet of the lorry. The old women were no longer let in to hunt for coal, I would meet them, with their blurred faces, and their stumpy legs wrapped in rags, wandering dazedly along the road, by the new barbed-wire fence.

As the year darkened so the house grew sombre, standing stark against a knife-coloured sky, a ragged flock of rooks wheeling above the chimney-pots. The first gales of the season stripped half the trees in the park, opening unexpected vistas. Indoors it was like being on a great ship at sea, the windows in their warped frames banged and boomed, and a grey, oceanic glow suffused the ceilings. Beneath the creaks, the rattlings, there was a deep, undersea silence. This was Sophie's medium. It was as if something had been left switched off, like the lights in a blind man's house. She was so quiet it was hard to find her. I would steal upstairs and along the corridors, my heart unaccountably pounding, and come upon her in one of the empty rooms, standing motionless at the window, her arms folded and her forehead pressed to the glass, so still, it seemed she must have been there for hours, without moving. Sensing me behind her, she would turn slowly, and slowly smile, blinking her dark, doll's eyes.

Often too I would find her with Mr Kasperl, sitting quietly in his room in an old deckchair, with her legs folded under her and her hands resting in her lap like a pair of pale birds, while he lay on the bed reading, or working at his charts. The room was dim and hot, like the lair of a large indolent carnivore. He would be in his waistcoat, collarless, his bootlaces untied. He took scant notice of me. His silence was profound, a far place where no one else could follow. Sometimes he worked in his notebook. He would frown over a page for a long time without stirring, then lean forward suddenly with a snort and inscribe a line or two, driving the pen heavily, with grim exactness. He let me see things, certain insoluble niceties, but in such elaborately casual, roundabout ways that it might all have happened by accident. He would leave the notebook open near me and wander off, padding here and there about the room, while I squinted avidly at the place where he had been working. It was always some paradox, some tautology. He was fascinated by things to which there could be at best only an inconclusive result. Strange geometries amused him, their curved worlds where no parallels are possible, where there is no infinity, where all perpendiculars to a line will meet in one mad point. He would come and stand beside me and consider these queer axioms, panting softly, and softly flexing his stubby fingers, and I would seem to hear, deep down within him, a faint, dark laughter.

I came away from these occasions in a sort of fever, my head humming, as if from a debauch. Things shook and shimmered minutely, in a phosphorescent glow. Details would detach themselves from their blurred backgrounds, as if a lens had been focused on them suddenly, and press forward eagerly, with mute insistence, urging on me some large, mysterious significance. A wash of sunlight on a high white wall, rank weeds spilling out of the windows of a tumbledown house, a dog in the gutter nosing delicately at a soiled scrap of newspaper, such things would strike me with strange force. They were like memories, but of things that had not happened yet. Walking home through the town on those smoky autumn evenings, past lighted pubs, and factory workers on bikes, and the somehow sinister bonhomie of fat shopkeepers standing in their doorways, I would feel a shiver of anticipation, not for what would be there now, the cosy hopelessness of home, but for that vast, perilous sea that lay all before me, agleam and vaguely shifting, in the dim distance.

One afternoon in November I spied Uncle Ambrose's car coming down the drive at Ashburn. I hid behind a tree while he went past. When I got home he was there, sitting bolt upright at the tea-table, looking about him with a stunned smile, his small shiny head swivelling slowly and his adam's apple bouncing.

– A what? my father was saying, with what in him passed for a laugh. A chauffeur?

Uncle Ambrose nodded, still dazedly smiling, amazed at his own audacity. He said:

– From Ashburn to Black's, just, and then out to the mine.

My mother had stopped behind him, and was staring at the back of his head.

– What? she said sharply. What? When is this?

Uncle Ambrose jerked his chin forward, working a finger in under the collar of his shirt.

– Oh, every day, he said. Monday to Friday. And bring him home again in the evening.

– Home, my mother said. Ha!

He took up duty straight away. He drove out to Ashburn each morning prompt at nine, and pulled up at the front door with a discreet toot on the horn. He would not venture into the house, but waited patiently in the car, sitting motionless behind the wheel and gazing off impassively through the windscreen, with an air of disinterested rectitude which he wore like a uniform. Often an hour or more would pass before Mr Kasperl appeared. Uncle Ambrose did not mind. He was nowhere more at ease than in his car. It was a huge, black, old-fashioned sedan with a long sloped bonnet and a humped back, like a hearse. On a few evenings, returning early from the mine, he stopped – it must have been at Mr Kasperl's bidding – and picked me up on my way out to the house after school. I sat in the back seat with the fat man, my satchel pressed on my knees. No one spoke. Mr Kasperl looked out his window, his arms folded and his stout legs crossed, puffing on a cigar. Now and then I would catch Uncle Ambrose's eye in the rearview mirror, and immediately we would both look away, with a guilty start. He drove very slowly, turning the wheel with judicious attention, like a safe-cracker. Each time he changed gear he would hold in the clutch for a moment, and the car would billow forward in a sleek, brief bound, rolling a little, and Mr Kasperl and I would be lifted up an inch and then dropped back gently on the high, soft seat. As soon as we had drawn to a stop at the house, Uncle Ambrose would slide out smartly and turn, in one continuous movement, twirling on his heel in the gravel, and snatch open Mr Kasperl's door, while I scrambled out the other side and hared off up the steps. Sometimes Felix made him drive me home as well. Those trips were the worst. I sat in the front seat, sweating, while Uncle Ambrose clung to the wheel in an excruciated silence, like a stammerer stuck in the middle of a word.

Felix seldom travelled in the car, preferring to walk, even in winter weather, with his hands in his pockets and his coat swinging open. But he was delighted with Uncle Ambrose, and studied him enthusiastically, this large swarth moist man, with his queasy smile and his tight suits and his aura of talcum powder and pain. On mornings when Mr Kasperl was late, Felix would come down and lean in the window of the car and hector him gaily, with roguish winks and jabs. Uncle Ambrose responded with a befuddled, panic-stricken grin, nodding and mumbling. Felix looked at me wide-eyed, in mock wonder.

– So many relatives you have! he said. Why, they're everywhere.

Aunt Philomena did not know whether to be jealous of Uncle Ambrose now, or proud of him. Ambrose, at Ashburn! Who would have thought it? Emboldened, she intensified her assaults on Mr Kasperl's stony solitude, but in vain, he sat alone with his thoughts by the window in the hotel dining room as he had always done, taking no notice of anyone. She turned to Felix then, lying in wait for him in secluded spots about the hotel, sitting up very straight with her neck stretched out and her lips pursed, a cup of coffee at her elbow, a cigarette with an inch of ash on it clipped tightly between two tensed, tremulous fingers. Felix listened to her attentively, with a bland, dreamy smile.

– Oh, Ambrose! she would say, with a dismissive sniff. The things I could tell you about poor Ambrose . . .

And she would gabble on, in rising tones of vehement sincerity, while a puckered skin formed on her coffee, and the ashtray on the low table before her sprouted a thicket of incarnadined butts, the least damaged of which Felix would save, and store away pensively in his tobacco tin.

The photographic studio, a winter afternoon, the gas fire hissing. I liked it here, the clutter, the quiet, the chemical smell, the grainy light that seemed, at this dead end of the year, to drift down from the ceiling, a strange, dense element, like pale smoke. Another world lay all around me here, a jumble of images. How sharp they were, how clear, these pictures from the land of the dead. I examined them minutely, one by one, as if searching for someone I knew, a known face, with blurred grin and unfamiliar quiff, looking up from that picnic table, in summer, in sunlight, among trees. I would not have been surprised, I think, if that face had been my own, so real did that world seem, and so fleeting, somehow, this one. Sophie, sitting by the fire, turned her gaze towards the door with an expectant smile. I had not heard a sound. Felix came in.

– Hello, Hansel, he said. Why, and Gretel too!

He looked from one of us to the other, grinning. He was carrying a white gown draped voluminously over his arm.

– See what I found, he said.

It was a wedding dress, elaborately embroidered, the heavy silk frayed and rusted with age. Sophie with a joyful yelp rose and took it from him, and held it against herself and laughed, turning this way and that. Felix put a hand to his heart and cried:

– Ah, thou still unravished bride of quietness!

He produced a crumpled white veil and placed it on her head with a flourish. She laughed again, her tongue rolling on her lower lip, and ran from the room. We heard her racing up the stairs and through the bedrooms, searching for a mirror. Felix chuckled, and crossed to the gas fire and rubbed his hands before the flame, his eyes lifted to the window. A fistful of rain swept against the glass with a muffled clatter. Rooks were squabbling outside in the darkening trees. He hummed the Wedding March, and grinned at me over his shoulder and softly sang:

> Here comes the bride,
> Contemplating a ride . . .

He chuckled again, and wandered idly about the room, picking up things and tossing them aside. He glanced at me slyly and said:

– What are you thinking about, bird-boy?

– Nothing.

I was thinking that I would always be a little afraid of him.

– Nothing, eh? he said. Well that's a lie, I know. You're thinking dirty things, aren't you?

He made a monkey face and crouched and capered, howling softly. I had to laugh. Sophie came back then, dragging behind her the trunk of fancy-dress costumes from the cupboard under the stairs. She had pulled on the wedding dress over her own skirt, and wore a battered top hat that Felix had found in the attic. The dress was too small for her, and hung askew, hitched on one hip, her wrists and ankles sticking out. She delved in the trunk and brought out a dusty tailcoat and a pair of striped grey trousers, and offered them to me. But Felix had other plans. He made a rapid sign to her, and she laughed, and pulled off the dress and gave it to him. He turned to me.

– Come on, sweetie, he said, you be the bride.

I backed away, but he followed me, laughing, and flung the dress like a net over my head. I shivered at the chill slither of silk. From the pleats and secret folds there rose a smell of camphor and of wax, and something else that was unnameable, a faint, stale, womanly stink. The bodice pinched my armpits, the skirts hung heavy against my knees. Sophie laughed and clapped her hands.

– *Salve*! Felix cried. *Salve, vagina coeli*!

He fixed the veil on my head, and Sophie produced a

lipstick and painted my mouth, frowning in concentration and biting the tip of her tongue. She rummaged in the trunk again and brought out a dainty pair of white shoes with high heels. She knelt before me and took off my shoes, and smiled up at me, cradling my moist heel in her hand.

– Tarra! Felix trilled. The slipper fits!

I ventured forward unsteadily in the spindly shoes, my calves atremble. I felt hot and giddy. A spasm of excitement rose in me that was part pleasure and part disgust. It was as if inside this gown there was not myself but someone else, some other flesh, pliable, yielding, utterly at my mercy. Each trembling step I took was like the fitful writhing of a captive whom I held pressed tightly to my pitiless heart. I caught my reflection in a cracked bit of mirror on the wall, and for a second someone else looked out at me, dazed and crazily grinning, from behind my own face.

– Radiant, Felix said, clasping his hands to his breast. Just radiant. Why, Miss Havisham herself was never half so fetching.

Sophie put on the clawhammer coat and tipped the top hat at a jaunty angle, linking her arm in mine. Felix bowed before us, blessing the air and mumbling.

– In the name of the wanker, the sod and the holy shoat, I pronounce you bubble and squeak. Alleluia. What dog hath joined together, let no man throw a bucket of water over.

He bowed again solemnly and closed his eyes, moving his lips in silent invocation, then turned his back to us and raised his arms aloft and intoned:

– *Hic est hocus, hoc est pocus.*

He farted loudly.

– *Nunc dimittis.* Amen.

Sophie pressed my elbow tightly to her side and leaned her head against mine, shivering with laughter. I was as tall as she in my high heels. I caught her warmish, lilac smell. Felix rubbed his hands.

– That's that, he said. Now for the photo.

He brought a wooden box–camera on a tripod and set it up in front of us, and bent and peered through the lens, wagging his backside and shuffling his feet.

– Watch the birdie, now! Snap! There.

He thrust the camera aside and danced to the door.

– Come, gentles, he cried. Come, Cinders, foot it featly now!

He flung open the door and backed into the hall with his arms lifted, conducting himself in song.

> Tum tumty tum!
> Tum tumty tum!

I tottered forward on quaking ankles. Sophie, weak with mirth, leaned on my arm, I thought we both would fall. I turned my head and kissed her swiftly, clumsily, on the corner of her mouth. She laughed, her breath warm against my neck.

– Ah–ah! Felix said, wagging a finger. No kissy-kiss! *Das ist verboten*.

He retreated before us, singing, and wildly waving his arms. Behind him, a man in a camel–hair overcoat came out of the library and halted, staring at us. Sophie dug her nails into my arm. In the sudden silence Felix stopped, and looked behind him, his smile turning to a smear. He let fall his arms.

– Why, he said under his breath, if it isn't Prince Charming!

He was a tall, sleek, black-haired young man with broad shoulders and small feet and a small, smooth head. He wore spectacles with thick lenses, which made his eyes seem to start forward in stern surmise. He had a big pale nose, and a little black moustache like a smudged thumb-print. His expensive black shoes were narrow, and highly polished. His fawn overcoat appeared somehow overcrowded, as if a tall man were crouched inside it with a small, imperious companion sitting on his shoulders. I struggled out of the dress and flung it behind me. He looked from my bare feet to Sophie's top hat, his eyebrows raised, then fixed his bulging stare on Felix and said:

– Mr Kasperl.

Felix made a sort of squirming curtsey, laughing breathily and kneading his hands.

– Oh, no, he said, no, I'm not Kasperl.

The stern eyes grew sterner.

– I meant, where is he? I know who you are.

Again Felix bobbed and laughed.

– Oh, I see, he said, I see. Well, he's at the mine, I'd say.

There was a pause. The tall young man put his hands in the pockets of his overcoat and looked about the hall.

– The mine, eh? he said.

He seemed sceptical. His gaze settled on the hanging strips of wallpaper and he frowned. He turned back to Felix.

– You know who I am?

Felix smiled obsequiously.

– Yes, I think I . . .

– D'Arcy's the name. I'm here on behalf of certain interests. You understand?

– Certain . . . ?

– Yes. Certain parties. I've just come down.

He kept his fish-eyes trained on Felix for a moment, with a forceful, meaning look. Felix tittered. There was another silence. Sophie stirred, and gave a little sigh, letting go my arm.

– Well then, D'Arcy said, suddenly brisk, let's have a look around, shall we?

He turned on his heel and marched up the hall. Felix made a face at his back, wagging his head and grinning, his tongue lolling. Sophie swept past him, and followed D'Arcy into the drawing room.

– Huh! Felix said. Behold the handmaid of the Lord!

In the drawing room she was opening the shutters. She turned to D'Arcy with a brilliant smile, as if she had let in the light for him alone. D'Arcy eyed her dubiously.

– And you, he said, what is your name?

She shrugged, still smiling. Felix coughed, and put a hand over his mouth and said:

– Deaf, I'm afraid.

A wrinkle appeared on D'Arcy's smooth pale brow.

– Deaf?

Felix nodded, assuming a sad face.

– As a post, yes. Dumb, too.

D'Arcy glanced in my direction.

– And . . .?

Felix nodded again.

– Very sad, he said. Very.

D'Arcy looked at him searchingly in silence for a moment, then turned abruptly and left the room. Sophie quickly followed him. Felix, bent double in soundless laughter, clutched my arm.

– Oh my, he wheezed, what a chump!

But he was not so blithe as he pretended.

D'Arcy had gone upstairs, with Sophie at his heels. We followed. D'Arcy strode from bedroom to bedroom, casting a disapproving eye about him at the dust and the disarray, breathing grimly down his nose.

– Do you people *live* here? he said incredulously.

Felix pointed a thumb at the ceiling.

– Up there.

– Up . . .?

– In the attic. This house has many mansions.

He laughed. D'Arcy's glance was cold.

– Oh yes? he said.

– Airy, you see. Wonderful views. And then, the stars at night, like . . . like . . .

D'Arcy walked to the window and stood looking out into the twilight, his hands clasped at his back. Behind him Felix made another grotesque face, put his thumbs in his ears and waggled his fingers, sticking out his tongue. Sophie frowned at him.

– This is not satisfactory, D'Arcy said almost mildly, as if to himself. This is not satisfactory, at all.

He turned to Felix.

– Is it? he said. Nothing done, no repairs, filth everywhere, people going about in rags, barefoot.

Felix smiled, holding out his empty hands.

– It's not paradise, I grant you, he said. But it does for us, sir.

– I'm not interested in what does for *you*, D'Arcy said, with a terrible stare.

We all went downstairs again, trooping in D'Arcy's wake. He stopped in the hall and took off his glasses and polished them on a spotless white handkerchief. His eyes sprang back into his skull, two tiny, bright beads. He peered at us sightlessly, the lenses flashing in his hands.

– And there have been reports, he said. Something or other about money, some sort of freelance dealing. I shall be making inquiries.

He put on his glasses solemnly and looked hard at each of us.

– You will hear from us, I don't doubt.

He advanced to the front door. Sophie was there before him, she opened it slowly, smiling eagerly into his face. He avoided her eye, and stepped out into the sodden dusk. His car waited on the gravel, a large, gaudy, gold machine, the roof stippled with rain. He buttoned his overcoat.

– Tell your Mr Kasperl, he said over his shoulder. He'll be hearing from us.

– Oh, I will, Felix said seriously, I'll tell him.

D'Arcy lingered, looking at Sophie's tailcoat, at Felix's attentive smile, at the traces of lipstick on my mouth. He was about to say something more, but a fat drop of rain from the guttering got down the back of his collar and he shuddered, his shoulder-blades twitching like wings. He turned and went quickly down the steps. Sophie waved until the rear lights of his car were out of sight down the drive. Felix scowled, grinding the fist of one hand into the palm of the other.

– How did he get in here, he muttered, that . . .

He saw me watching him, and grinned.

– Trouble up mine, eh? he said, winking. And up theirs, too.

I HAD A DREAM OF D'Arcy, a huge figure descending slowly through a hole in the roof at Ashburn, swaddled in his rich, blond coat, his glazed eyes staring and his arms clasped on his breast. Rain fell after him through the gaping hole, and dead songbirds and twigs and bits of paper. Now, I thought, now everything will change, will end. But nothing happened. One day a letter came for Mr Kasperl, in a thick white envelope with D'Arcy's name and the address of a firm of solicitors embossed on the flap. Felix held it to his ear and shook it gingerly, in mock trepidation. Mr Kasperl read it impassively and tossed it aside. Sophie reverently retrieved it. Among the marionettes lined up along the wall in her room, one had acquired an overcoat and painted-on glasses, and a rudimentary wig of black wool slicked down with glue.

My mother heard of D'Arcy's visit from Uncle Ambrose. She nodded grimly. He would soon settle their hash, she said. Oh yes. She looked about her for agreement, then frowned, and turned away. Everyone was against her. First

Aunt Philomena had deserted her, then Uncle Ambrose. Jack Kay's dying had been a dereliction too. And now she was alone. She never mentioned Ashburn or its tenants by name, it was always *that place*, and *them*, her tensed mouth turning white. Then people fell silent, and looked at their hands, as if she had said something foolish, or tasteless, and they were embarrassed for her. How could they not understand? Something was being destroyed, trodden underfoot. She thought of the past. As a girl she had worked in a draper's shop in the town. She had been happy in that dim sanctuary. The raw texture of life as she knew it in the cottage at Ashburn had given way here to the softness of silks and stuffs. The polished counters, the brass fittings, even the mirrors, had a satin feel under her fingers, sumptuous and cool. She had liked best the early afternoons, when business was slow, and she was free just to stand in the midst of all that peace, listening to the hushed voices of the other assistants gossiping in the linen department, while at the far end of the shop the draper, a plump man with half-glasses, drew out bolt after bolt of cloth and unfurled them with a deft flick of one white hand, beaming over his spectacles at the customer before him, who stood, in seamed stockings and a feathered toque, humming thoughtfully, a finger pressed to her cheek. But she liked too the Saturday late openings, when everything was noise and bustle, and the wooden cylinders on the overhead cables whizzed back and forth from the cash office, and the air was laced with a genteel tang of sweat. Haberdashery had been her department. She had a counter to herself, fitted with many minute drawers and glass panels and velvet display cases, like an elaborate toybox.

She would finger dreamily the trinkets in her care, the spools of thread, the buttons, of ivory, bone, mother-of-pearl, the packets of pins and ranked, gleaming needles, and think of that paradise of grace and ease she had glimpsed across the green lawns of Ashburn.

Then she had married, and one day at the beginning of spring the draper called her into his private room behind the cash office. She stood motionless before his desk, trying to hold in her already burgeoning stomach. She watched his lips move. He would not meet her eye. When he had finished she said nothing. He threw his pencil down on the desk.

– After all, he broke out petulantly, this is a fashion shop, my girl, and look at you!

She walked the long length of the shop, trailing her finger on the counter, to the door and the grey, March day, feeling a flash of pain inside her like a flaming sword.

These are the things she thought about, these are the things she remembered.

On my way out to Ashburn I would stop sometimes at Coolmine. I liked to wander among the dust-hills and the lakes of broken glass, there was something grimly satisfying in such a wide expanse of waste. The lorries from the factories had built up a ramp of sand and rubble, down the steep sides of which I would wade, feeling a thrill of panic as the whole bank for yards around began to shift and slide. All sorts of things surfaced in these slippages and slowly sank again into the churning rubble, rusty springs and die-punched metal plates, and volutes of steel shavings with pleated edges and a nude, subterranean gleam. The tinkers had got in again. Something had happened to them, though. They did not hunt for scrap metal any more, but sat about in dazed huddles, fighting and weeping, and drinking out of big brown bottles. They would shout at me as I went past, calling me a fucking cunt and offering me a drink. They had ravaged faces, and maddened, bloodshot eyes. Occasionally one of them would heave himself up and hobble after me, trying to tell me something, waving a ragged arm. I remember their mouths, soft, shapeless holes, like half-healed wounds.

Work at the mine was going slowly. There had been roof-falls and flooding. The men were not happy, I would meet them trudging home at evening, begrimed and sullen, the whites of their eyes flashing. Felix was fed up.

– Time to move on, he said. Nothing left here. Look at it.

We stood on the edge of the ramp, above the pit-head. Men were coming up out of the hole, others were going down. The lorry sat drunkenly at the side of a dirt track, where it had broken down one day, never to go again. We could see Mr Kasperl sitting in the cab, with his charts and his cigar. A grey wind swarmed up the ashen slope, bringing us a whiff of sulphur from the railway yards beyond the road. Off in front of us there was a broad salt marsh, and beyond that, in the distance, the sea. All wrong, though, surely, this geography, or do I mean topography? It doesn't matter. Felix beat his hands together in the cold.

– Yes, he said, time to get out.

We walked along the ramp. Below us, at the foot of the

slope, a trickle of water slid between banks of smooth blue mud. Once I had seen a kingfisher there, a flash of opalescent silk, skimming the surface. Today the water reflected an iron sky.

– What about you, bird-boy? Felix said. Fancy coming with us? You could be with your Leda. We could go, oh, anywhere. Foreign parts. See things. Wild horses on the plain of Muscovy, camel trains in the Sahara. The jungle, nigger girls stamping around a fire stark naked. Or what about the far north? Eskimo women are slippery as eels, they'll put their tongues anywhere.

He laughed.

– What do you say?

I said nothing. We went down the slope and along the track in the direction of the gate. I was thinking, I was thinking about – oh, nothing, I was thinking about nothing. Suddenly Felix laughed out loud and clapped me on the shoulder.

– Oh, Malvolio! he cried. Your face!

Mr Kasperl was eyeing us through the murky windscreen. Felix waved to him gaily.

– Get away from him, too, he said, his beck and call.

He took my arm.

– And you, he said, you should get away from him as well. Seriously, I mean it. He's too . . . too negative. Me, now, I'm for positive things, rules, order, certainty. That's how we're alike, you and me. You don't believe me? Well, you'll see. The world is wide. I have plans.

We heard the explosion then, or felt it, rather, a sort of shiver under our feet. For a moment afterwards all was still.

– Oops! Felix said softly, and snickered.

A confused shouting arose. A puff of smoke climbed rapidly into the air above the pit-head, turning itself inside out. It looked oddly festive. Mr Kasperl was scrambling down from the lorry. Figures had begun to totter on rubber legs out of the mouth of the mine. We ran towards them. I wanted instead to run away, but I could not stop myself. How vivid the blood looked, on their blackened faces. They were making an odd, wailing sound. A man whose trousers had been blown off knelt in the mud, weeping, his hands clasped as if in prayer. Another stood and cursed, swinging his fists at anyone who came near him. I noticed he had lost an eye, there was just a purplish mess where it had been. Smoke was pouring out of the mine, and down in the depths someone was screaming steadily, in short bursts, like a baby, going ah! ah! ahh! Mr Kasperl stood stiffly atop a hillock of shale, in a statuesque attitude, fists clenched at his sides and head thrown back, looking at the scene about him with an expression less of shock, it seemed, than a sort of scepticism, as if it were all a show got up to fool him, and he had seen through it. He turned a suspicious eye on Felix, who lifted up his hands and stepped back with a laugh, shaking his head.

– Don't look at me, boss, he said. I have an alibi.

Some sort of gas had exploded in one of the tunnels. Two men had been killed, a dozen were maimed. The story was in all the papers. They misspelled Mr Kasperl's name. Felix was not mentioned, which provoked one of his rare bouts of rancour. For days he would speak to no one, but kept a sullen, injured silence.

SPRING CAME EARLY that year – no, I'm wrong, it came late. But when it came it was glorious. I recall the jonquils blowing on the lawn at Ashburn. All work at the mine had stopped. The roof supports rotted. People said the place was haunted, ghostly rumblings were heard underground, and sometimes at night a bluish radiance was seen flickering above the pit-head. Each morning at nine Uncle Ambrose arrived in his car and sat outside the house for an hour, and then drove slowly, sadly away again. Mr Kasperl kept indoors, creaking up and down the stairs and through the empty rooms. I would come across him in odd corners, standing motionless, like a stalled automaton, glazed, absent. A sort of paralysis had settled on him. He would sit in his room with the black notebook open on his knees, staring blankly at the pages. He looked strange, not like the rest of us. He might have come from a country where no one else lived.

One morning early I arrived in the attic and found Felix crouched in the corridor outside Sophie's room. He put a finger to his lips and pointed. Her door was ajar. She was still in bed, lying on her side, with a hand under her cheek and her eyes closed. A luminous white mist pressed in the circular window above her, lit by a pale sun. Her clothes were draped untidily on a chair beside the bed. Mr Kasperl stood a little way from her, as if sunk in thought, palping his fat lower lip with a finger and thumb. Outside, under the eaves, a pigeon sounded its soft, lewd note.

– Watch! Felix hissed gleefully, gripping my wrist. Watch now!

Mr Kasperl took a step forward to the side of the bed and paused, watching Sophie's face. Then, laboriously, his boots groaning, he knelt down by the chair and gathered her clothes in his arms and buried his face in them, snorting softly. Felix let slip a little moan of laughter, and clapped a hand to his mouth. Mr Kasperl was oblivious, nosing deep in the bundle of silks, devouring their secret fragrances, his fat old shoulders trembling. Sophie had opened her eyes, and lay unmoving, watching him. Now she looked towards the door and saw us there, our faces pressed to the crack. She smiled.

– Oh, look at him, look! Felix whispered in ecstasy. Oh, the dirty old brute!

Felix too was lying low. There had been a row at Black's, when relatives of one of the men who had died tried to attack him, and he had to escape out the back way. He was indignant. Why were they after him? It wasn't his fault.

Probably one of those dolts – maybe that very Paddy or Mick himself, or whatever he was called – had lit up a fag down there. But feelings were high in the town. My mother listened to the talk, and decided the time had come to act. I arrived home one evening to find her ironing her best dress, her white cotton gloves, banging the iron down on the board with angry strokes. Uncle Ambrose was there, flushed and frowning, staring at the floor and trying to control the jitters in his knees. My father cocked a wary eyebrow.

Next morning Uncle Ambrose called for them in his car. My mother was already waiting, sitting by the window in the parlour, with her handbag and her hat and her white gloves. It was a Sunday in May, I remember the sun in the window, the heavy reek of her face powder. My father, shaved and brushed, limped down the stairs, muttering. Uncle Ambrose wrung his hands unhappily. He cast a furtive glance at me, his adam's apple working. We had both been seduced by Ashburn, after all. He seemed strapped into his tight suit. The three of them stood on the pavement in the sunshine for a moment, confused a little by the light, the gay breeze, the trees delicately coming into flower. Then Uncle Ambrose led the way to the car, and settled himself in the driving seat with his accustomed care. He held the steering wheel at arm's length, as if he were afraid of it, and pumped the pedals and fiddled with the choke while the others got in. My father sat beside him, my mother took the back seat. She was saying something to me, but the window was shut, she could not work the winder, then the car shrieked as Uncle Ambrose trod on its underparts, and the last thing I saw, behind the reflected stage-set sliding on the glass, was her blurred face speaking without sound as she was borne away.

It was Aunt Philomena who came for me. At first I thought she was drunk. Her mouth was askew, and a strand of hair hung across her cheek. When I opened the door she was already speaking. Her voice was thick with what I took for manic laughter.

– I don't know a thing! she warbled. They phoned me up, they wouldn't tell me a thing!

We hurried through the town. The Sunday streets were deserted. A blinding disc of sunlight bowled along beside us in the shop windows. Aunt Philomena tottered on her high heels, sweating and muttering.

– *Are you a relative*? she kept saying. *Are you a relative*? that's what they asked me. A relative, indeed! The cheek!

The hospital was a big white building on a hill, impressive in the spring sunshine, like a grand hotel in some southern clime, its windows awash with the sky's festive blue. Another species existed here, different altogether from Aunt Philomena and me, fragile, etiolated beings, ennobled by their secret wounds. Even the visitors coming down the steps had a special air – thoughtful, solemn, a little dazed – as if they had gone in tipsy, but were sober now. The entrance hall smelled of tea and floor polish. At the reception desk a nun in an elaborate, winged head-dress was writing in a ledger. Aunt Philomena and I waited, standing on the gleaming parquet in the midst of a huge silence. Presently a nurse arrived, a tiny person with red hair and pretty, pink-rimmed eyes, and a watch on a strap pinned to her breast. I noticed her neat white shoes. She told us her name, which I forgot immediately, and shook hands with us tenderly. Her hand was warm and dry, she pressed it into mine like a little present, looking at me in silence, with a kind of gentle fervour. She led us down a corridor and up a curving flight of stairs. A wide window looked out over the town to a distant strip of dark-blue sea. A life-sized statue of the Saviour stood in a niche on the landing, glumly displaying a ruby-red heart in flames. The face was that of a bearded lady, creamy, smooth and sad.

We entered an enormous ward filled with light and noise, like a gymnasium. My father and Uncle Ambrose lay on their backs in adjoining beds, still and pale as a pair of marble knights. Each had his right hand resting on his heart, and his left arm extended at his side and connected by a tube to a bottle on a stand. Their skulls were wrapped in bandages. They breathed lightly in unison. Uncle Ambrose's nose jutted up out of his face like a stone axe-head, I had never noticed it was so large. He opened his eyes and looked at Aunt Philomena and me with a mild air of surprise.

– Mr Swan! the nurse shouted with startling force. You have visitors, Mr Swan, look!

But he made no response, and after a moment closed his eyes again with a fluttering sigh.

My father calmly slept on.

A doctor appeared, a stocky young man with restless

eyes and a lank lock of fawn hair lolling on his brow. He had
been at his tea, there were crumbs on the lapels of his white
coat, and his breath smelled warmly of cake.

– Windscreen, he said, smacking a fist into a palm. Like
that. They were lucky. Big black dog, he says, ran right
under the wheel.

Aunt Philomena turned aside with a strangled sob,
crushing a wadded handkerchief to her mouth. The doctor
looked at his shoes and frowned. In a bed in the opposite
aisle a large elderly man in striped pyjamas sat and watched
us intently out of an inflamed, avid eye.

– Well, the doctor said briskly, you'll want to . . . ?

Aunt Philomena, still chewing her hankie, shook her
head violently, giving another muffled sob.

I followed the doctor out of the ward, down the stairs
past the simpering statue and the panoramic window. The
rumble of tea-urns and the clatter of crockery came up
through the stairwell. The doctor went heavily ahead of
me, his knees working outwards like elbows and his white
coat billowing. He told me his name, but I forgot that one
also. A hunchbacked porter in a green hospital coat walked
past the foot of the stairs. The doctor called out to him and
he stopped and looked up at us warily, one hand resting
lightly in his coat pocket, as if it were holding a gun. He had
coarse oiled black hair, and thick glasses with heavy rims
that seemed a part of him, like a bony armature growing
out of his skull.

– Whassa? he said.

The doctor spoke to him quietly, and he nodded and led
us away down a corridor, taking from his pocket an
enormous bunch of keys on a metal ring. I could not take

my eyes off his hump. We entered a curving, dull-green passageway with little round windows like portholes set high up in the wall, and came to a grey metal door, where we stopped and waited while the porter sorted through his keys. The doctor hitched back his coat and put his hands in the pockets of his trousers.

– Sunday, he said, with an apologetic shrug. They lock up everything.

The door swung open on a small, high room lit by a dangling bulb. A large press with steel doors was set into the wall. The porter threw it open, revealing three chilled corpses neatly stacked on sliding shelves. I looked at the tops of their heads, their bleached ears wreathed in wisps of frosty smoke. The porter leaned down and read the name-tags on the shelves, screwing up his eyes behind their thick lenses and baring his side teeth.

– No, he said, not there.

He shut the press and slouched into a farther room, beckoning us to follow. There was a sink in the corner, and a desk with a stool, and a tiny window through which there streamed an incongruous thick gold shaft of sunlight. Our shoes squealed on the rubber floor. A trolley. A shrouded form. The doctor belched softly into his fist.

– There's a formality, I'm afraid, he said, in a confidential tone. Identification. We have to have it, in a case like this. You just say it is her, and that's it. Right?

The porter folded back the sheet.

– Now, he said, giving a professional little sniff.

The woman on the bier did look somewhat like my mother. She was older, she had a narrow forehead, and her hair was different too, but there was a resemblance, all the same, and for a moment I did not know what to think. Could it be that this really was my mother, and they had arranged her face all wrong somehow? Was that why they needed me to identify her, so they could make the necessary readjustments? I shut my eyes. No, no, impossible. Then there was the problem of what to say. Embarrassment opened its jaws and breathed its hot breath in my face. I felt a fool, as if in some way it were all my fault. The moment stretched, thinner and thinner. The doctor was beginning to fidget. I stepped back a pace. I had to cough to get my voice to work. No, I said, no, I did not think, there must be some, this was not . . . The doctor blinked.

– Not . . . ?

– My mother. No.

He turned swiftly to the porter, who scratched his head and frowned. Then he opened his mouth.

– Oh, jay, he said, hold on.

He crossed the room, and from behind a screen, almost with a flourish, he wheeled out on its rubber wheels another trolley, on which my mother's body was laid, wrapped in a tartan blanket. Her hands were folded. She was still wearing one white glove. Her face was turned aside, her cheek pressed against her shoulder. Her eyes were not quite closed. I could see no marks of the crash save for a small cut on her forehead. But there was something in the way she was lying, all bundled up like that, as if she had been snatched up and shaken violently, and everything inside her was broken and in bits. I caught a faint whiff of her face powder. The doctor was hovering at my shoulder. I nodded dully, identifying what was not there, for this was not my mother, but something she had left behind, like a mislaid glove.

Things are confused after that. There are gaps. I remember sitting in a cramped little room, a dispensary, I think it was, with a mug of grey tea going cold in my hands. There were coloured posters on the wall beside me, showing cross-sections of lungs, and seething stomachs, and an enormous, crimson heart with all its valves and ventricles on show. I felt a deep calm, as at the end of some daring and exhausting exploit. Part of my mind had been working away by itself all this time, suddenly now, as if out of nowhere, a solution to one of the equations in Mr Kasperl's black notebook came to me, in three smooth transformational leaps, tumbling through the darkness in my head like a spangled acrobat executing a faultless triple somersault. In the corridor Nurse Er was talking to Doctor Blur. Without warning I began to weep. It was like a nosebleed. My sobs were a kind of helpless, inward falling, as if a huge hollow had opened up inside me and I were plunging headlong into it. The storm ended as abruptly as it had begun. I wiped my eyes, startled, a little sheepish, and yet obscurely proud of myself, of such lavish, all-embracing grief. Then the doctor went off, and I followed him. We climbed the curved staircase again. It was evening already, I could hardly believe it. A vast, garish sunset was sinking on the horizon, like a disaster at sea. My father and Uncle Ambrose were still sleeping. Aunt Philomena's face was blotched and crooked. She leaned on my arm and we left the ward. The entrance hall was ablaze with thick sunlight. The nun with the head-dress was gone, had winged away, leaving the ledger open on the desk. No, there was no nun, I invented her. We walked home slowly through the deserted streets. The sky was pale blue, ribbed with red, so high, immensely high. Aunt Philomena snuffled and sighed. I wanted to get away from her. The trees were in blossom in the square, pink and ivory, purest white. A crow flapped past low overhead, clearing its throat. The key was under the mat.

SHE WAS BURIED IN the old cemetery at Ashburn, in the same plot as her mother and Jack Kay. I walked behind the hearse. It was a hot, hazy day, one of the first of summer. The hawthorn was heavy with may, and there was columbine in the ditches, and poppies, and wild honeysuckle. People turned up whom I had never seen before, big broad-beamed women in ugly hats and elasticated stockings, and gnarled old men, agile as woodsprites, who jostled for position among the over-grown tombstones, eager not to miss a thing. A shovel was stuck at an angle in the mound of clay beside the grave. The priest was a short, stout, florid-faced man. His voice rose and fell with a querulous cadence. All about us the fields sweltered. The air was laden with fragrances of hay and dust and dung. Aunt Philomena wept loudly, standing with shoulders hunched and her elbows pressed to her ribs, as if to keep something from collapsing inside her. My father and Uncle Ambrose stood side by side at the foot of the grave. Their bandaged foreheads gave them a faintly piratical air. Uncle Ambrose smiled to himself and murmured under his breath. The crash had damaged something in his head, it would never mend.

I looked about for Felix, but if he was there I did not see him.

They all came back to the house, the fat women and the old men, and sat in the parlour drinking stout and cups of tea and eating plates of cold meat that Aunt Philomena had prepared. There was an atmosphere of subdued levity. It was like a party from which the guest of honour had gone home early. Aunt Philomena had brought in a bunch of my mother's roses from the garden and set them in a bowl on the table, they hung there in our midst, nude, labiate and damp, like the delicate inner parts of some fabulous, forgotten creature. Uncle Ambrose was perched on an upright chair in a corner, with his hands on his knees. He was like a big, amiable boy dressed up for the occasion in someone else's three-piece suit. He kept peering about him with a crafty little smile, his lips moving silently. It was as if he had been let in at last on some great secret that everyone save he had always known.

– *Gone soft*, Aunt Philomena whispered, her eyes wide. She could not suppress a tremor of excitement in her voice. Here was drama more lavish than even she would have dared to dream up.

At last the mourners went away, and a huge, astounded silence settled on the house.

Aunt Philomena came up from Queen Street every day to take care of my father and me. At first she was all briskness, going at things with her sleeves rolled up, but soon the strain began to show. Uncle Ambrose was not getting better. They had taken the stitches out of his head, they told her he was all right, but still he would only sit and smile, communing with himself in a kind of happy wonderment. There were days when she had to get him up and dress him. He had bouts of incontinence. She fed him with a spoon.

– I don't know what to do! she would say. I don't know what to do.

And she would sit down suddenly, whey-faced, and light a cigarette with a hand that shook.

My father kept to the parlour now. Hours drifted past, white, slow, silent, like icebergs in a glassy sea. The bandage on his brow had been exchanged for a wad of lint stuck on with a criss-cross of pink sticking-plaster. His asthma was bad, the air whirred and clicked in his chest like the sound of a rusty clock preparing to chime. His hands gripped the armrests of his chair, his slippered feet were planted square on the floor. He was attentive, poised, as if he were waiting for someone to come along and explain things to him, how all this had happened, and why.

I sat at the table by the window in my room, with my head on my hand, as in the old days, what seemed to me now the old days. I lived up there. I would find scraps of forgotten food under my bed, or kicked under the wardrobe, rotted to an enormous pulp and sprouting tufts of blue-grey fur. The room developed a rancid, fulvous odour. I opened the window wide. Air of summer flowed over the sill, vague, silky, like air from another world. I worked, lost in a dream of pure numbers. How calm they were, how quiet, those white nights of June. I would look up and find the day gone, the night gathering intently around me, breathless and still aglow. I was a sleepwalker, waking in strange light in a garden of eyeless statues, confused, heartsore, wanting again the interrupted dream. There all had been harmony, the wilderness tamed, sundered things made whole. There too, somehow, I had not been alone.

Oh, I worked. Ashburn, Jack Kay, my mother, the black dog, the crash, all this, it was not like numbers, yet it too must have rules, order, some sort of pattern. Always I had thought of number falling on the chaos of things like frost falling on water, the seething particles tamed and sorted, the crystals locking, the frozen lattice spreading outwards in all directions. I could feel it in my mind, the crunch of things coming to a stop, the creaking stillness, the stunned, white air. But marshal the factors how I might, they would not equate now. Everything was sway and flow and sudden lurch. Surfaces that had seemed solid began to give way under me. I could hold nothing in my hands, all slipped through my fingers helplessly. Zero, minus quantities, irrational numbers, the infinite itself, suddenly these things revealed themselves for what they really had been, always. I grew dizzy. The light retreated. A blackbird whistled in the glimmering dusk. I held my face in my hands, that too flowed away, the features melting, even the eyeholes filling up, until all that was left was a smooth blank mask of flesh.

The weather turned strange, mists all day and not a breath of wind, the sun a small pale disc stuck in the middle of a milky sky. At evening the mist became drizzle, covering everything with a seamless coating of grey froth. All night the foghorns boomed and groaned out at sea. Something was happening underground. Tar melted in the streets, fine cracks appeared in the pavements. Gardeners turned up smoking clods of earth seething with grubs and fat slugs and ganglia of thick, pink worms. Vegetation ran riot. Huge mushrooms appeared everywhere, on lawns, under hedges, in the troughs between potato drills, pushing their way blindly up through the tepid clay like silvery, soft skulls. A rank smell clung in the air. Miasmas hid the salt marsh at Coolmine. When the tides were high the pit-mouth spouted geysers of blackened steam. Rumours went around of sudden fires, mysterious subsidences. A child playing in his grandmother's garden fell into a flaming hole that opened in the ground beneath him, and was found, singed and shrieking, clinging to the exposed roots of a tree, his legs dangling over the burning maw.

I traipsed the town, day after day. I saw D'Arcy's car, and then one day D'Arcy himself, sitting grimly by the window in Black's, in the place where Mr Kasperl used to keep his morning vigil. I began to go out the Coolmine road again. I saw the spot where Uncle Ambrose had crashed the car, halfway to Ashburn. A stone was knocked out of the wall, a telegraph pole was grazed. It was so little damage, I was surprised. The lorries were using the dump again. The gates had fallen down, the old women with their sacks were at work once more among the slag-heaps.

I went to Ashburn, of course. I skulked about the grounds, avoiding the house, as I used to do. Then one day I met Sophie, as I knew I would. She was walking under the trees. She had a straw basket on her arm, covered with a cloth. She was thinner, her face was paler, the eyes sunken. But she smiled at me as brightly as ever, as if she had seen me only yesterday. We walked up to the house. I carried her basket. It was filled with nettles.

Felix was sitting at the kitchen table, with his back to the doorway, singing.

> It is no secret
> What God can do,
> What he's done to others
> He can do to you . . .

He turned as we entered, and seeing me he grinned his foxy grin, and threw up his hands and cried:

– Why, look who's here! Bring me the fatted calf, at once.

He took out his tobacco tin and lit up a butt, examining me with friendly attention. He was wearing his greasy pinstriped suit and a deerstalker hat. A red silk scarf was knotted at his throat. On the table a carriage clock stood with its back open and innards on show. He pointed at it and said:

– Think I'd get anything for it?

Sophie was putting the nettles into a saucepan with water and a bundle of bones. He laughed ruefully.

– You see what we're reduced to.

He picked up the clock and shook it ruefully, producing a faint shimmer of sound, like a distant tinkling of tiny bells.

We ate the nettle soup. A lozenge of sunlight trembled on the table by my wrist. Sophie, smiling, watched me over her spoon. Mr Kasperl came in heavily and sat down. He looked at me once and then away. Felix talked and talked.

– Burning away merrily down there, apparently. The whole town is sitting on it. There'll be hell to pay. Oh, hell to pay!

He grinned at me.

– What do you say, bird-boy? Time to fly?

Sophie cleared the table, and Felix suggested a game of cards. Three of us played, while Mr Kasperl sat by, his fat arms folded and his chin sunk on his breast. A car came up the drive. Felix put a finger to his lips. We heard loud knocking at the front door, and D'Arcy's voice calling out. After a while he went away. Felix played a trump. He said:

– The common flea, or *pulex irritans*, which is the name we scientists call him, can survive alive a long time without food. He likes a spicy drop of good red blood, of man or maiden, it's all one to him. He doesn't bite, you know, for fun. In fact, he doesn't bite, but, rather, pricks, sucks up a ruby drop, and off he kicks. His cousin, *xenopsylla cheopis*, or rat flea, is a different type, for this lad does not at all like human gore, indeed, it makes him puke, which is a bore for such a lively fellow. But when his host, the black rat, *rattus rattus*, gives up the ghost, he has no choice but to go after us.

The poor chap's little proventriculus gets all bunged up with swarming bacilli, whose name is *pasteurella pestis*, need I say any more? Now, dying for a feed, he subjugates his loathing to his need, and finds a human target double quick. In goes the sharp proboscis, and the trick is done, a drop of blood is aspirated into the proventriculus. Now sated, our Jumping Jack relaxes, but, oh dear, some of that blood comes up again, I fear now rife with bacilli, and goes straight down the puncture hole. The victim, with a frown, scratches the spot, while *pasteurella pestis* heads pell-mell for the region of the testes. A week elapses, then the buboes swell, there's fever, stupor, and, of course, a smell as if the poor wretch were already dead. Next wifey gets it, baby too, then Fred the postman, yes, and Fred, the postman's son, then in a twinkling half the town is gone. It flies like black smoke, felling frail and fit, soon continents are in the grip of it. And all the doing of his majesty, our lord of misrule, Harry Hotspur Flea! So now, remember, when you feel a bite, it really is an honour, not a slight. The king is dead, long live the prince, and – and there's the knave! My trick, I think. And hand.

Sophie put on a marionette show. She had cleared a work-table in the photographic studio and rigged up a stage made from cardboard boxes. The insides of it were lined with pictures. There was the imperial baby, and the donkey with the straw hat, and the gentleman in leotard and the naked lady astride the chair, her plump legs splayed. Felix bent to examine her, and gave a low whistle and nudged me.

– Aye aye, he said, this will be good.

The marionettes jerked and clattered, bowed and swayed. The strings seemed not to guide but hinder them, as if they had a flickering life of their own, as if they were trying to escape. It was my story they were telling. Everything was there, the meeting above the meadow, my first meal with them, D'Arcy's visit, Jack Kay, the kiss, everything.

– Top hole! Felix cried, clapping like a seal. Oh, top hole!

Sophie stepped from behind the table and bowed. Mr Kasperl stood in the doorway, his arms dangling. Sophie went to him.

I walked with Felix in the grounds. A weak sun shone out of a white sky. The trees glistened, oiled with mist. I could smell the sea, its grey stink. Felix was munching a crust of bread. He wore his deerstalker, and a dirty, dun mackintosh, and a bedraggled tie with stripes.

– My going-away outfit, he said. Like it?

He flung the crust away. An enormous seagull swooped down out of the mist on thrashing wings and caught it in midair. Felix ambled along in silence for a while, sucking his teeth.

– Yes, he said, have to get out. That mine . . .

He brooded a moment, then suddenly giggled.

– The small investor, I've discovered, lacks a sense of humour. A poor loser, all round.

He halted, and turned to me. We were standing on the drive. The tops of the trees were hidden in the mist.

– Listen, he said, you like to know the truth, don't you?

In the beginning was the fact, and all that? Well, come on, then, I'll show you something.

We went into the house, up to the attic, to Mr Kasperl's room. Felix quietly pushed the door open an inch. I put my eye to the crack. The room was full of calm white light. A fly buzzed against a window-pane. Mr Kasperl lay on his back on the bed, eyes closed, his mouth open, like a big, beached sea-creature. His legs were unexpectedly skinny, with knotted, purple veins. His big belly glimmered palely, rising and falling, lightly flossed with reddish fur. His sex lolled in its thick nest, livid, babyish and limp. Sophie stood at the foot of the bed, putting on her slip. She lifted her arms above her head, for a second before the silk sheath fell I saw her shadowed armpits and silvery breasts, the little patch of black hair between her legs. She turned then and caught sight of me. She smiled, and came towards us, with a stocking in her hand. I stepped back, and Felix deftly closed the door.

Downstairs he fished in the sagging pocket of his mackintosh and brought out the carriage clock and peered at it.

– Dear me, he said, is that the time?

A battered cardboard suitcase stood in the hall. He picked it up.

– Well, I'm off. After summer merrily, you know. Care to walk me to the train?

ON THE COOLMINE ROAD he whistled, swinging the suitcase jauntily. Smoke rose from the pit-head into a sky as pale as pipeclay. A lorry was going in at the gate with a load of broken bricks. A band of tinkers trudged along the edge of the bank of rubble, forlorn dark figures against the white sky. The gleaners were busy. Bundles of mist hung above the marsh. Felix stopped to survey the scene. He raised one arm in a sardonic salute and said:

– Farewell, happy fields!

We passed by the broken wall, the scarred telegraph pole. He pretended not to notice, and said nothing.

The streets of the town were damp, and smelled of sea-slime. There were not many people about, but all the same Felix went forward circumspectly, keeping on the inside, near the wall. At Black's he paused.

– Time for a last look in, you think? he said. Oh yes, come on, let's risk it, if you will so will I. I'm an old sentimentalist, I know.

We sat at Mr Kasperl's table by the window. Felix turned his back to the street, hiding his face with his hand. I told him how I had seen D'Arcy here. He shrugged.

– Oh, him, he said, don't worry about him. He's only a messenger boy.

The waitress came, a raw-faced country girl. Felix rubbed his hands. He was peckish, he wanted a fry.

– Rashers, he said. Sausages. Nice bit of liver.

The girl grinned at him in fright, biting her lip.

– I'm not supposed to serve you, she said.

Felix stared indignantly.

– Eh?

– Miss Swan says . . .

– Miss Swan? Miss Swan? You tell Miss Swan I'll see her myself presently.

She hurried away, still nervously grinning. Felix winked at me. I looked out at the street, past our faint reflections on the window. He touched my arm.

– I say, old chap, don't fret, he said. Not worth it, believe me. Forget what's gone, that's my motto. Cancel, cancel and begin again.

I was not jealous, not really wounded, even. I felt excluded. Through that crack in the door I had glimpsed a world, subtle, intricate, unsuspected, where I could never enter. Felix lighted up a butt and smoked in silence for a while, glancing at me with a contrite air.

– It was for your good, he said. Besides, you could have had her too. The hints I dropped! Still, you're better off out of it, with that one. I should know, it was me that found her for him. That was the kind of job I had, is it any wonder I'm getting out?

He met my eye, and tittered.

– Yes, I know, he said shamefacedly, I found you for him too, didn't I.

I thought of the marionettes, twitching on their strings, striving to be human, their glazed grins, the way they held out their arms, stiffly, imploringly. Such eagerness, such longing. I understood them, I, poor Pinocchio, counting and capering, trying to be real.

Felix rapped the table angrily with his knuckles and stood up.

– Well! he said loudly, if they won't serve me, I won't stay!

He threw his cigarette butt on the carpet and ground it under his heel, and took up his suitcase with a haughty flourish. In the doorway we met Aunt Philomena, with the grinning waitress behind her. Felix stepped back a pace, lifting his hat.

– Ah, he said, with a weak laugh, Miss Swan, so there you are.

She stood frozen-faced, her hands gripped before her, looking at the floor beside his feet. Me she ignored. There were crumbs of face powder clinging to the bristles at the corners of her mouth. She dismissed the waitress with a twitch of her shoulder. Her knuckles whitened. She said:

– There's a matter I want to discuss with you.

Felix gave her his blandest smile.

– But of course, he said. Only, not now. In a hurry. Train to catch.

There was silence. She would not budge out of the doorway. Still with her eyes fixed on the floor she turned her peremptory shoulder an inch in my direction. I

squeezed past her. The waitress, loitering in the lobby, gave
me a conspiratorial wink. Behind me Felix was saying:

– What? Savings? What? Oh but my dear, I'm sorry, that
was in the nature of an investment, I thought you understood. You're not the only one, after all . . .

I waited in the street, and presently he came out, shaking
his head.

– Phew! he said. See what I mean? No sense of humour.
They can't wait to get in on a thing, then the first minute it
goes wrong they bring out the knives, bawling for their
pound of flesh.

He laughed, and clapped me on the shoulder.

– But not you, eh? he said. No, not you.

We walked up Owl Street, under the flying spire. The
hens were squawking in the poulterer's yard. Before us the
town drifted in the mist.

– Come with me, Felix said, why not? We could be a pair,
you and me. He says you have a great future, really brilliant.
He'd know, he had a brilliant future too, one time. Ha!

He led me along Goat Alley, down the slimed steps, to
the quayside. The sea was calm, mud-coloured.

– By the way, he said, I brought you something.

He opened the suitcase on his knee, and brought out Mr
Kasperl's big black notebook.

– Keep it, he said. As an awful warning. And listen, take
my advice, stay clear of him. He's finished. His time is up.
The two of them, finished.

We reached the station. His train was in. He skipped
nimbly aboard, swinging up his case, and turned and leaned
out the window. The whistle blew.

– Goodbye, he said, winking. *Auf Wiedersehen.*

Then the train started with a jolt, and he was carried away down the platform, waving, smiling, past the signal box, and the signal, and into the long, descending curve of Coolmine.

Cancel, yes, cancel, and begin again.

Ashburn was silent. I walked through the empty rooms, under the high, shadowed ceilings. A broken shutter, rotting floorboards, a prospect of trees. In the studio the marionettes lay where Sophie had left them, asprawl under their cardboard canopy. How cleverly she had managed the likenesses, D'Arcy's hair, Uncle Ambrose's shiny head, my blank mask, and Mr Kasperl's eyes, those blue eyes that watched me now, impassive as ever. No, not impassive, but as if from a great way off, so far away he could hardly make me out. She was the same, that same remote gaze. She was smiling. She rose to her feet with a rustle, a muffled clatter. Mr Kasperl hung behind her, breathing. I spoke. They could not answer. How could they answer? How silent everything was, suddenly, teetering there on the brink. Then a kind of thrumming began under my feet, faint at first, growing rapidly louder, a great drum-roll out of the earth. The floor sagged, groaning, and with a crash collapsed. The fat man and the girl sank slowly, as if into water instead of flame. His blue eye. Her smile. My hair was on fire. A red roar came up out of the hole, and I flew on flaming wings, clutching my black book, through smoke and dust and splintering glass, into the huge, cold air.

II

ANGELS

O LAMIA, MY DEAR, my darling, Lamia, my love. How diligent you were, how well you cared for me. I can see you still, your smooth skin of tenderest mauve, your insides white as white, your name in wonderfully clear, minute print, and that coy little letter R, enclosed in a ring, like a beauty spot on your glossy cheek. You melted under my tongue, you coiled yourself around my nerves. What would I have done without my Lamia, how would I have borne my season in hell? There were others that ministered to me, but none that gave such succour. Here is Oread, white nymph of forgetfulness, and Lemures, the deadeners, like little black beans, and skittish, yellow-hued Empusa, hobgoblin to the queen of ghosts. They are angels of a lesser order, but precious for all that.

I slept, it was a kind of sleep. Deep down, in the dark, an ember of awareness glowed and faded, glowed again. A word would enter, or a flash of light, and ramify for hours. I was calm, mostly, feeling nothing. Outside the dome of numbness in which I lay I sensed something waiting, like an animal waiting in the darkness. That was pain. Pain was the beast my angels kept at bay.

They came to me, my guardians, in endless file down their transparent ladder, into my arm, when at last I opened my eyes I saw the sun shining in the plastic bag above me, a ball of white fire streaming outwards in all directions. The room was white, a thick cream colour, really, but it seemed white to my eyes, so accustomed by now to black. Splinters of metallic light coruscated on walls and ceiling, like reflections from a glittering sea.

Water. The thought of water.

At first I was a mind only, spinning in the darkness like a dynamo. Then gradually the rest of me returned, rolling up its sleeves and spitting on its hands with the grim enthusiasm of a torturer. I watched the liquid in the plastic tube, a fat tear trembling on its steadily thinning stalk. Then the stalk snapped, the drop fell. Pain pounced.

How to describe it? Not to. I was Marsyas, lashed to my tree, the god busy about me with his knife, whistling through his teeth as he worked. I was alone, no one could help me. The difference, the strangeness. This was a place where I had never been before, which I had not known existed. It was inside me. I came back each time a little more enlightened. Now for the first time I saw the world around me radiant with pain, the glass in the window suffering the sun's harsh blade, the bed like a stricken ox kneeling on its stumps, that bag of lymph above me, dripping, dripping. The very air seemed to ache. And then the wasps dying, the moths fumbling at the window, the dog that howled for a whole night. I had never known, never dreamed. Never.

The loneliness. The being-beyond. Indescribable. Where I went, no one could follow. Yet someone managed to hold my hand. I clung to her, dangling above the abyss, burning.

Never known, never dreamed.

Never.

Scorched hands, scorched back, shins charred to the bone. Bald, of course. And my face. My face. A wad of livid dough, blotched and bubbled, with clown's nose, no chin, two watery little eyes peering out in disbelief. Yes, they let me see myself. That was later. They gave me a hand mirror, I wonder where it came from? It was round, with a pink plastic handle and a back in the fan shape of a sea shell. I don't think, no, I don't think it belonged to her, though it was she who put it into my swollen paw. When I had finished marvelling at my face I angled the glass downwards, and was dazzled by the glare of metal.

– Tinfoil, Dr Cranitch said. To prevent heat loss. A new technique.

But that was later again.

I liked the nights. The silence was different than by day, when it was not really silence, but suspension, as if things around me were holding their breath, appalled, speechless with wonder. At night a great nothingness blossomed like a flower. The room was faintly illumined. When I turned my head, when I was able to turn my head, I could see the open doorway, and then another room, or a corridor, in darkness, at the far end of which there was a desk, and someone sitting at it, dressed in white, who never moved, but kept her vigil all the long night long. A green-shaded lamp stood on the desk, throwing its rays downwards, only her shoulders and the sleeves of her white coat could be seen, and something around her neck that shone. A path of light lay along the polished floor, like a shimmer of moonlight on black water.

By day my door was kept shut. I strained to catch the vague hubbub from beyond it, voices and footsteps, the hum of machinery. There was a stairs nearby, and overhead people walked up and down. How busy they seemed! Once someone cried out, a long, desolate wail that rose up and up, like a red rocket, then wavered, and sank back slowly to a gurgle. That was the apogee of those days, the day of the scream. I was not alone.

I howled too, making someone else's day, no doubt, bringing him a little solace, a sense of companionship. It was clear then I would survive: if I could scream, I would live. She came running at once, on her rubber soles, and emptied an ampoule of double-strength Lamia into my dripfeed. It was night when I woke again. She was at her desk, as always, headless in the lamplight. I imagined it was always she. All hands were her hand, all voices her voice. It was a long time before I began to distinguish the others, to distinguish them from her, I mean. I took scant notice of them in themselves. It was she who had kept me alive. She held on to me, and would not let go her grasp, until at last I scrambled up, out of the pit.

Weeks, weeks. I could feel the summer passing by outside, the slow days falling, one by one. At evening the visitors came. I heard them traipsing along the corridors, their heavy, swinging tread. I thought of a religious procession. Sometimes I even caught a whiff of the flowers they brought. They did not stay long, and passed by again, with a lighter step. A few stuck it out until the bell went. Then the tea was brought around, the skivvies singing. A mutter from the chapel as the rosary was recited. I listened, hardly breathing. I thought of the others, for I knew there must be others, straining like me after these last sounds, these last few drops, dripping into the sand.

Now I could not sleep, I who had slept for so long. I built up walls of number, brick on brick, to keep the pain out. They all fell down. Equations broke in half, zeros gaped like holes. Always I was left amid rubble, facing into the dark.

Father Plomer visited me. I opened my eyes and there he was, sitting beside my bed, with his legs crossed under the shiny black skirts of his cassock and his large, pale, hairless hands clasped on his knee. He smiled at me, nodding encouragingly, as if he were a hypnotist, and I his subject, coming out of a trance. I could not see his eyes behind the flashing lenses of his spectacles. He leaned forward, with a confidential air, and spoke softly.

– And how are you, young man?

– I want to die, I said.

– What's that?

I tried again, getting my blubber lips around it.

– Die, I said, I want to die.

– Oh now. They tell me you're doing fine.

In sleep the sirens had sung to me, I could still hear their sweet song.

– Don't die, the priest said, and smiled blandly, gently wagging his head at me. Not a good idea.

The nurses were cheerful, cheerful and brisk, or else preoccupied. Not she. She moved with slow deliberation, saying little. Her hands were broad. She was young, quite young, or not old, at least. It was hard to tell. They laughed at her behind her back, called her a cow. She spoke to them quietly, in a stiff, formal tone, never looking at them directly. Yes, matron, they would say primly, their lips tightening. And she would turn away. Her face was covered with freckles, big coffee-coloured splashes, the backs of her hands too. She wore a cross on a fine gold chain around her neck. It dangled above me the day she cut me out of my metal wrappings. It took a long time. She plied the scissors and then the swab, turn and turn about. Her face was impassive, fixed in concentration. I could hear no sound anywhere around us, as if the whole hospital had been emptied for the occasion. Full summer sunlight streamed in the window. A nickel dish glinted. The tinfoil crackled, a cocoon breaking open. I wept, I moaned, I pictured a ribbon of raw, red stuff winding endlessly out of my mouth. Dr Cranitch appeared above me, his hands in the pockets of his white coat.

– Well, he said. You've pulled through.

A RIVEN THING, incomplete. Something had sheared away, when I pulled through. I was neither this nor that, half here, half somewhere else. Miscarried. Each day when I woke I had to remake myself, build myself out of bits and scraps, of memories, sensations, guesses. I knew how Lazarus must have felt, standing in the blinding light of noontide in his foul cerecloths, with a headache, confused, suspicious, still vividly remembering the other place, unsure that it was not better there than here.

– You were lucky, Dr Cranitch said in his jaded way. Full-thickness burns like that, they destroy the nerves.

– But I can feel, I said.

– What? Where, show me.

He hitched up his glasses and peered where I pointed.

– No, no, he said. Impossible. That's phantom pain.

He sat beside my bed on a swivel stool. He was on his rounds, he wore a tweed suit, a tie with a narrow knot. Tall, thin, pale as a sea-washed bone. An air of remote amusement. That wan smile, as if he were remembering an old and feeble joke. He laid his cool hands on me, turning me this way and that, a sculptor with a dollop of clay. The blind was down, the air was close.

– We're very hopeful, he said. Aren't we, matron? Yes, very hopeful.

She said nothing. A sharp breeze fingered my flayed back.

– Tomorrow, then. Tomorrow we make a start.

I remember the steely clink of instruments, the sharp, chemical smell, the cluster of faceted lights above me, like a bright sun shining through rain. I was conscious through it all, day after day. The atmosphere in this high room had a curiously neutral feel, as if the air itself had been treated with a mollifying gas. At intervals one of the nurses would remove Dr Cranitch's spectacles and wipe the lenses, while he stood vague-eyed, his hands limply lifted. Then he would lean over me again, deft, mild, faintly abstracted, sometimes humming under his breath. His students looked on, stealthily jostling. I thought in amazement of people outside in the streets, going heedlessly about their business. So I too, before, while worlds thrashed in agony.

Grafts. Forceps. Gauze. Such words, I tremble still.

Now came a new kind of pain, pain's big brother, it caught me in its burly grasp and pulled me this way and that, it would brook no nonsense, even my ministering angels threw up their hands before its masterful onslaught.

This was recovery.

– Yes, Dr Cranitch murmured, it's knitting nicely.

I could not lift my left arm higher than my shoulder, my right was a hinged brown stick. I had no nipples. Half the skin of my stomach had gone to patch my legs, my back. My face now was a glazed carnival mask, with china brow and bulging cheeks, hawk nose, dead eye-sockets. Above it the skull was a tufted leathern helm, the skin taut and glassy, like dried-over slime.

– It will heal, Dr Cranitch said. As good as new, almost.

But I was different. I was someone else, someone I knew, and didn't know. I had stepped into the mirror. I frightened myself. That mad face. Those eyes.

My first, faltering little steps. I shuffled crabwise to the door, hands flapping in fear, stood panting there, eyes shut, then in panic staggered headlong back to the bed, missed it, fell on the floor. Followed by a quaking bout on the bedpan. For a minute, though, I had forgotten the pain. It came back now, bounding and barking, and licked my livid face into flame again.

She held my hand, my elbow. Her mannish grasp. She watched my feet, in old grey felt slippers, inching along.

– Come, she said quietly, under her breath. Come along.

What a pair we must have been, this big, broad, sad woman, and I, bent and hobbling, hairless as a babe.

– Can't. Can't.

Stopped, stood still, would not go on, or back. She waited, saying nothing, she had seen it all before. We reached the window. She parted the venetian blinds, the crackle as the blades bent made me grind my teeth. Bright sunshine outside, a bank of barbered grass sloping away to railings and a wall, then in the distance the city shimmering in a blue haze. The city! Too much, too much. At the window-sill a fuchsia bush with wasps. Too much. I lay down on the floor and sobbed, pressing my pitted cheek to the cool rubber tiles.

– Come along, now. Come along.

Her freckles, my burns.

I began to explore my little world. There was a wooden locker beside the bed, a metal chair, a waste bin lined with a plastic bag. In an alcove there was a washbasin, and a mirror screwed to the wall. A rich, deep, silver crack ran athwart the glass, slicing my face diagonally in two from temple to jaw. The locker was empty, except for a shrivelled brown apple core and a holy medal on a pin. And the black notebook. The cover was scorched. I shut the door on it.

Miss Barr was a big blonde person with ruddy cheeks and prominent, pale blue eyes. She wore a white tunic and starched white trousers, and white ankle-boots with thick crêpe soles. Her straw-coloured hair was tied back tightly in a knot, I imagined her, first thing out of bed each morning, gathering it up and giving it a good, hard wrench, stretching the skin at her temples, making those eyes bulge. She smelled of soap, lint, liniment. I used to

dream about her. My sleeping self quailed before her, weak
with anticipation of exquisite harm. The first day she
came into my room she rolled up her sleeves and said
briskly:

– Right, my man. Physio for you.

I thought she was mad, I did not know what she was
talking about. She seized my arm, my leg, peering.

– Golly, she said, you certainly made a bags of yourself.
But fear not, we'll soon set you to rights.

We heaved and hauled together, like decrepit wrestlers,
groaning. She had a tendency to fart. She told me about her
childhood, spent mainly among horses. At once I pictured
her, a sort of centaur, flying over the greensward, snorting.
Sometimes I pictured myself too, astride her, the breeze in
my face, hearing the thunder of hoofs, feeling her great
heart hammering under me. She put her knee in my spine,
sat on my chest, bent me over her shoulder.

– Pull, pull! she shouted. Get those sinews stretched!
We'll make a new man of you yet.

The day I left my room. That was a day to remember. I sat
cross-legged on the bed, with my hands in my lap, my eyes
fixed on the door, then saw myself, as if it were someone
else, rise and turn the handle and walk out. A long, low
ward lined with beds, with figures in them, sitting up and
looking at me. All those eyes! I had expected a vast
emptiness, huge halls, the odd, solitary figure turning
away. A small man in slippers and a sort of smock
approached me. Smoked skin, sallow eyeballs, a lick of

greased black hair. He greeted me with easy familiarity, grinning on one side of his sharp little face.

– Well well, he said, our mystery man.

He led me along the beds, introducing their occupants. He did not ask my name. He was a card, with a brisk line in raillery. Old chaps chortled, young ones smirked. All tried not to see me, my scabs.

– I'm for the knife, myself, he said, indicating the smock.

Some beds he passed by in silence. Bandaged skulls, wax faces, dazed, impenetrable eyes.

– Brain cases, he whispered darkly. You want to watch them.

His name was Sykes, Stokes, something like that. He offered me a plum from a bag on his locker.

– Had an accident, did you? he said.

Next day when I came out he was gone. The sheets had been stripped from his bed, the door of his locker stood open. Only a plum stone remained, stuck to the bottom of a tin ashtray. The knife had done for him. My cicerone. No, my Virgil. For this is hell, after all.

Sighs, groans. Shouts in the night. An old man puking up gouts of green stuff, leaning over the side of the bed, a young nurse holding his forehead. Slow, wet coughs, like the noise of defective suction pumps ponderously labouring. In the huge, white-tiled bathrooms, little labels exhorting patients not to spit in the handbasins. Everywhere the same thick cream paint, smooth as enamel, clammy as skin. I wore a mouse-coloured dressing-gown with faded red piping. Someone had died in it, I imagine, before it passed to me. I walked and walked, slouching along the vermiform corridors, dragging one foot. People looked away from me, visitors especially, the uninitiates. Young doctors frowned, a sort of bland grimace, as at a show of bad taste. I passed on, hauling my pain behind me.

Pain had a smell, flat, grey, faintly sweet, I imagined a mixture of scurf and faeces. It was how I recognized my fellow sufferers, the ones for whom pain was a constant presence, a sort of second, ghostly self. There was the silence too, a special kind. We would sit in what was called the recreation room, a group of us, doing nothing, not saying a word, and yet communing somehow, like participants in a seance.

There were times when I fancied I was only this ectoplasm, floating, transparent, invisible to the hale. One day I found my way on to the maternity ward, and stood at the glass wall of the nursery, gaping at the rows and rows of prune-faced mites in their plastic cots, and was for a moment baffled, an old ghost stumbling on a new world. They looked like me! I pressed my forehead to the glass, yearningly. A mother in a pink bed-jacket glanced up from her babe and shrieked, and I was led away, shaken, speechless, that one foot dragging behind me, in the grave.

I thought of all my dead. I thought of Sykes, or Stokes, who had gone under the knife. He was not anywhere any more. Oh, part of him was still about, in the morgue, probably, and probably still in better shape than I, with half my flesh fallen from the bone. But the rest of him, that grin, the sharp glance, the jokes, where was all that? Gone. That was death. No cowled dark stranger, no kindly friend, not even empty space, with all the potential that implies, but absence, absence only. The nothing, the nowhere, the not-being-here. But how then this something, wafting me onwards irresistibly, as if all around me a great, slow breath were being indrawn?

– Don't die, Father Plomer said. Not a good idea.

He sat beside the bed, regarding me gaily, with his legs crossed, swinging one large, black-shod foot. He was the hospital chaplain. He had an aura of shaving balm and warm wine.

– Of course, he said comfortably, life is a wretched thing, and practically worthless. Yet we must live, all the same.

I was tired of him, his big smooth face and plummy voice, his genial detachment.

– For what? I said.

To laugh was complicated, with my face, I did not do it often. He smiled, compressing his lips, as if he were nibbling a tiny seed in his front teeth.

– Why, he said, to practise for the eternal life to come!

Now it was his turn to laugh, he leaned back, his glasses flashing, ha, ha, haa! A vision came to me of his face peeling from the skull, the crimson flop, the sinews, gleet, glint of bone, the eyeballs wallowing.

– I think we have a young pagan here, matron, he said. Oh yes, I shall have to take him in hand.

She stopped behind him and looked at the back of his head in silence for a second, then turned away. He laughed his laugh again, a series of soft, plosive puffs, his lips pursed as if he were blowing smoke rings.

He taught me to play chess. He had a plastic travelling

set, we balanced it between us on the edge of the bed. It did not take me long to learn. It was a kind of moving geometry. He played a ramshackle game, swooping about the board, making sudden, lunging moves and then taking them back again with a giggle, only to get himself at once into a worse muddle.

– You're better now? he said to me, frowning over a tangle of pawns. Improving, I mean? Check, by the way. Or is it? No.

He stared owlishly at the board, humming unhappily under his breath. His last remaining bishop made a bolt for freedom. He had not noticed my knight.

– Yes, he said distractedly, life, life is the . . .

The knight reared, slewing sideways, stamped to a stop.

– Mate, I said.

He gave a little shriek of surprise, throwing up his hands.

– Why, so it is! he cried, laughing. So it is!

Go out, they told me. Take a walk, yes. Go into the city, see the sights, mingle. Simple, ordinary things. It's all there, waiting for you, your birthright. Be one of the living, a human being. They gave me clothes, a shirt, shoes, trousers, a coat. When I dressed I felt a sort of excited revulsion, as if I had put on not only someone else's outfit, but someone else's flesh as well.

ON THE HOSPITAL steps I stopped. A high gold autumn evening was sinking over the rooftops. Forever after I would think of the city like that, like a waste of magnificent wreckage, going down. My hands shook, stuffed into these unaccustomed pockets. Such space, such distance. I was dizzy, I felt that if I fell I would fall upwards, into the limitless air. A panic of disconnected numbers buzzed in my head. Grass, trees, railings, the road. The road! A bus hurtled past, swaying on the bend. It might have been a mastodon. The evening visitors were arriving. I turned my face away from them and plunged off down the drive.

Oh, that first autumn. Vast tender skies, branches soot-black against blue, a sense of longing and vague hurt in the dense, luminous air. I wandered the streets like an amnesiac, everything was new and yet unaccountably familiar.

I recall especially that brief hour at the exhausted end of evening, when the shop workers had gone home, and everything was shut, and a mysterious quiet settled everywhere. Then the beggars and the drunks came into their own, the dustbin-pickers, the frantic old women who lived out of shopping bags, and those ragged but strangely robust young men with blue chins and crazed eyes, marching headlong down the middle of the pavements, swinging their arms and furiously muttering. They seemed to know something awful, all of them, some secret, the burden of which had blighted their lives. And I was one of them, or almost. An apprentice, say. An acolyte. I stalked them for hours, loitering behind them on canal bridges, or under archways, where the pigeons strutted, and dust and bits of paper swirled in eddies, and everything was spent and grey and heart-breaking. I can't explain the melancholy pleasure of those moments, from which I would turn away lingeringly as the last light of day drained down the sky, and the street lamps came on fitfully in the blued autumnal dusk.

Oh, the squares, the avenues, the parks. A smoky, sunlit morning, smell of washed pavements, fish, stale beer. A carthorse clops past, dropping dark-gold dungballs. Snarl of traffic. A sudden dark wind, making the day flinch. Then rain. In the park the dripping trees circle slowly around me, halt when I halt. The spidery dome of the bandstand teeters, threatening. Sun again, a drenched glare. Stop on this corner, by this bridge. A butcher's shop, a greengrocer's, a red-brick bank like a child's toy house, with gold lettering in the windows and a big hanging clock. A workman with a ladder strapped to his bike waits at the traffic lights, whistling. A lorry shudders to a halt with a gasp of brakes.

What is it, this sense of something impending, as if a crime is biding its time here, waiting to be committed? The lights change. I detect the slow ruin of things, the endless, creeping collapse.

And then the nights, silver and burnished black, the shadowed buildings crouched under a tilted moon. A neon sign flicks on and off, on and off, in strange silence. Somewhere a woman laughs. In a windswept street by the river two old men in rags are fighting. They caper weakly, panting, swinging their arms, their coat-tails flying. Thick smack of fist on flesh and one goes down, the other takes aim, kicks, again, then hard again. The wet street gleams. A newspaper blows along the pavement, plasters itself against a grille. A huge seagull alights on the road, fixing me warily with one round eye. I pause in a doorway, wait, eager and afraid. Some dirty little truth is being wearily disclosed here. The gull flexes one wing, folds it again. The tramp on the ground coughs and coughs, holding his face. The other one has run away. Foul breath of the river, dark slop of waters, slide, and slop again. Hush! What conjured spirit . . .? Hush!

I was sitting on a park bench when I met him, when he met me. It was an October twilight, the grass was grey with dew. I was listening to the trees, their fretful rustlings. He walked past once, came back and passed by again, returned again more slowly, stopped. Thin foxy face and widow's peak and thin, sly smile. He put his hands in his pockets, arched an eyebrow.

– I say, he said, do I not know you?

He studied me, my bird-boy's profile.

– I never forget a face, you know.

He chuckled. I was not surprised to see him. He sat down beside me, settling the wings of his old coat. I told him my story. He listened, motionless, hands folded on one bony knee. Darkness advanced across the park. The bells of the city were ringing, near and far.

– All that time in the bonehouse, eh? he said. But look at you now, a new man.

A bat flitted here and there above us in the violet air.

– Help me, I said.

He gazed out over the darkening sward, nodding to himself.

– Oh, Caliban, he said, you should have come with me when I asked you. Didn't I tell you it was all finished there, didn't I warn you? And see what happened.

He sighed. A band of masked children ran out of the bushes, shrieking. I put a hand up to my face.

– Help me.

– You want to be a real boy, eh?

He sat back on the seat and crossed his legs and gazed up into the shadowy branches above him.

– We had some fun, didn't we, all the same? he said. High times. It seems so long ago, now, all of it. Still at the sums?

– Yes.

The laughing children returned, and ran in a circle around the bench where we sat.

– I think they want you for a guy, Felix said.

He rose, and they fled away into the bushes. He stood a moment, looking about him pensively in the dusk. Then he produced a scrap of paper and a pencil stub and scribbled an address and handed it to me.

– I'm there sometimes, he said. In the evenings. It's not far.

He walked off a little way, stopped, came back.

– You see? he said. I told you, I never forget a face.

Chandos Street was a decaying Georgian sweep with a Protestant church at one end and a railed-off green square at the other. I loitered there night after night, pacing under the streetlamps, watching the house, one of a tall terrace, with worn granite steps and a black front door. People came and went. No, no one came, no one went, the door never opened. Sometimes a lame whore sat on the steps, tipsily singing. Once she asked me for a match, and called me a cunt when I said I had none. We were not the only loiterers. A couple appeared on the corner by the church, at the same time every night, a sick-looking young man with the shakes, and his shivering wraith of a girl, straggle-haired, with matchstick legs. They would hang about for an hour, peering anxiously up the ill-lit street, then turn and shuffle away miserably. The young man took to saluting me, touching a jaunty finger to his forelock and trying to grin. One night he stopped me, put a shaky hand on my arm and looked behind him carefully, as if he were about to impart some valuable secret. Instead he asked me for money. The girl stared blankly at my midriff. I gave him a handful of Empusa tablets. He looked at them in wonderment and whistled softly.

– Fucking ace, pal, he said. I'll offer up a novena for you.

And there was another girl, skinny also, with skinny legs and a pinched face and pale, narrow wrists. She wore a plastic raincoat and white shoes, and clutched a white plastic handbag. She smoked cigarettes, and paced from one trembling patch of lamplight to another, watching the street, the houses. She ignored me. The young man with the shakes approached her, his hand out, she ignored him too. She smoked and paced, smoked and paced. One night I tried to follow her. After we had gone a street or two she turned aside suddenly and jumped on a bus. I shrank back in the darkness and watched as she was borne past me, sitting up very straight at the window, her sharp little stark white face and cropped, crow-black hair.

At the end of a week Felix appeared at last, strolling up the street with his coat open and his hands in his pockets. The girl walked across swiftly and accosted him on the steps. He stopped with his finger lifted to the bell and retreated a pace. She spoke to him quietly, fiercely. I crossed the road and stood below them on the pavement. The girl immediately fell silent. Felix looked over his shoulder.

– My dear fellow, he said, there you are.

The girl turned an inch in my direction, but kept her eyes lowered. There was a silence. Felix glanced from one of us to the other.

– Are you together? he said. No? What a coincidence, then.

He rang the bell, but no one came. He rang again. We waited. Then the girl, with a furious gesture, opened her bag and produced a key. Felix grinned at her. She ignored him, jabbing the key into the lock.

A gaunt, dim hall, olive walls, a dirty lightbulb in a brown paper shade. The stair carpet was threadbare. In silence we ascended into the gloom. Felix smiled to himself, whistling softly. The girl walked ahead of us. Her hair stuck up in tufts at the back, as if someone had tried to pull it out in handfuls. She knocked at a door on the third floor, but it was only a gesture, she had a key for here as well. Inside was dark save for a faint sodium glow seeping down through the tops of tall windows. Felix switched on a light.

– What ho! he called. Are you there, truepenny?

No one answered.

There were cardboard boxes on the floor inside the door, and piles of books, and a black overcoat and an umbrella hanging on a peg. The kitchen smelled of gas and oilcloth and something going bad. Felix lit the stove, opened a cupboard. The girl walked into the front room. I followed her. She stood at the window looking out. The church spire loomed in the dark against an acid sky. Clutter here as well, more boxes, books, soiled plates on the table. The girl was lighting a cigarette. The match flame shook.

– You followed me, she said. That night.

She went on looking out the window. Her mind seemed to be on something else.

– You shouldn't follow me.

Felix came in, carrying a teapot.

– Now! he said brightly. Nice cup of tea.

He was wearing an old raincoat and scuffed, sharp-toed

shoes. He set the teapot down on the table, sweeping aside smeared plates and scattered cutlery.

– Getting acquainted, you two, I see, he said.

He carried three cups to the fireplace and emptied their dregs into the littered grate.

– I don't want any of that stuff, the girl said.

He frowned, looking about him in exaggerated puzzlement.

– Stuff? he said. Stuff? Oh, the tea, you mean. Oh.

He laughed to himself and went back to the table, shaking his head. He poured three cups of tea, and handed one to her. She took it.

– Did you know, he said to her, our young friend here has been in hospital too. Did he tell you?

For the first time now she looked at me directly. She had small, dark eyes, close-set, with a slight cast. She studied me for a moment, biting her lip. Her plastic raincoat was buttoned to the throat.

A door behind us opened, and a small, fierce-looking man came in. He was wearing long woollen underwear, with a blanket draped over his shoulders. His hair stood up in sprouts of ginger bristles, and he had three or four days' growth of reddish beard. He began to say something but sneezed instead. His bare feet were small, with horny, yellow nails.

– Ah, professor, Felix said. We thought you must be out.

The little man glared at him.

– I am sick, he said.

As if for emphasis, he sneezed again violently. Felix pointed to the blackened pot on the table.

– Some tea, professor.

This time the little man ignored him. The girl had turned back to the window. He hitched up his blanket, looking at her, and then at me.

— Who are you? he said.

Felix coughed.

– This is the one I told you about, he said. You remember.

The professor opened his mouth and squeezed his eyes shut. We waited, but the sneeze did not come.

– Ah, he said sourly. The prodigy.

His name was Kosok.

HAVE I MENTIONED the buses? I liked them, the way they trundled through the streets, gasping and shuddering, like big, serious, labouring animals. I would board one at random and ride to the end of the line, hunched in the front seat upstairs, watching the city unfurl around me, the tree-lined avenues and the little parks, the domes and turrets and curlicued façades. A hoarding would slide past, then a burnished stretch of river, then a dead-end street with parked cars and children playing ball under a rusted railway bridge. I got to know the top half of things, the shabby upper storeys of smart shops, the fire escapes, the pots of geraniums in little sooty windows, the faded signs on brick walls for carbolic soap and plug tobacco and ship's chandlers. And then the suburbs, the windswept wastes of housing estates, with straggly gardens, and toddlers dabbling in the gutters, and the sudden, quicksilver flash of a mirror in the drab depths of a bedroom window.

When I think of those aimless, dreamy journeys, I think always of the girl. When she left the flat that first night

I went with her. We walked through the dark streets in silence. When the bus came we were the only passengers, except for a drunk slumped on the bench seat at the back. We watched the glossy darkness sliding past the window. She smoked a cigarette. Her name was Adele. She looked at me sharply.

– I'm not a Jew, you know, she said. You needn't think I'm a Jew.

The conductor told her she was not to smoke. She paid him no heed. She held the cigarette aloft in her thin, white fingers, flicking the end of it with a bitten thumbnail. We went by the river, under the jagged shadows of warehouses and cranes. The drunk woke up and shouted for a while, then fell into a stupor again. The conductor walked up and down between the rows of seats, chewing a matchstick, getting a good look at us, my face, her frantic hair, grinning to himself. Adele kept her eyes fixed on the window, flicking her cigarette, flicking, flicking, vibrating faintly, as if a thin, continuous current were passing through her.

– I hate him, she said. That hair. The way he walks, as if he had no backbone.

I knew who she meant.

Suddenly she laughed, a brief, psittacine cry. Then she frowned, and stood up quickly and pressed the bell. The drunk mumbled in his sleep. We alighted at a deserted corner, under a leaning lamp. There was a bit of broken wall painted blue, and a high rickety wooden fence with things scrawled on it, names and curses and hearts with arrows in them, and a bulbous, cleft woman drawn in chalk. Adele looked about her with a preoccupied expression, clutching her handbag to her narrow chest. Her lips were black in the lamplight. The silence of the night arranged itself around us.

– Is this where you live? I said.

She looked at me in surprise.

– No, she said. Why?

A dull pain throbbed in my right arm, like an old dog yanking at the leash. I swallowed a pill.

– Where do you get them, she said, those?

I offered her one. An Oread, the last of my supply. She examined it, and put it in her mouth and swallowed it carefully, as if it were not a pill but a bit of my pain itself I had given her. For a second time she looked at me directly.

– Gabriel, she said. Is that your name?

She never smiled. She had only that laugh, and now and then a sort of grin, wild-eyed, distraught. There was a bus coming on the other side. She put her head down and walked away from me quickly across the road, the heels of her white shoes tap-tapping the asphalt. The headlights of the bus caught her briefly. She got on board and it churned away, trumpeting, into the darkness.

I went down the quays again next morning, but everything looked different by day, I could not find that corner with the blue wall and the wooden fence. The cranes and the blank sides of the warehouses had the look of things turned away, smirking in derision.

Felix came with me to the hospital for my weekly visit. We had to wait a long time, sitting in a row of wooden benches in the outpatients' hall. There were mothers with cowed children, raw-faced young men in suits, and doll-like girls with impossible hairstyles, their mouths painted scarlet. All stared before them with the same expression of mingled boredom, disbelief and fear. At intervals a door in front of us would open and a nurse would appear and call out a name, and a boy in splints would get up, or a rheum-eyed old fellow with the shakes, and shuffle forward meekly. Then all would shift, sliding sideways, and the one at the end of each row would nip into the place vacated on the bench in front. Felix laughed.

– Like a little chapel, he said. And we're all going to confession.

He sat at ease with his legs crossed and one arm draped along the back of the bench, smiling about him at the whey-faced coughers and the painted girls. He nudged me and whispered:

– What a bunch, eh?

When my turn came he rose eagerly to accompany me, but the nurse prevented him. He got to the threshold of the consulting room, and managed a good look inside before the door was shut in his face.

– Such cheek! the nurse said.

But she smiled all the same.

The place was busy as always, assistants in white coats walking about hurriedly with files under their arms, the consultants at their tables, magisterially bored, half listening to whispered tales of frights and night-sweats and sudden, astounding pains. An old chap was being weighed, standing atremble on the scales, clutching the waistband of his trousers in a bony fist. In a curtainless cubicle a fat old biddy sat on the side of the bed fumbling with her suspenders, while a nurse stood by, tapping one foot. Dr Cranitch looked at me blankly, then consulted his file.

– Ah, yes, he said. Swan. How is it?

I showed him my arms, my shins. The grafts had held, new skin was spreading, a roseate lichen. He nodded, humming. I asked him for a prescription. He pursed his lips and looked past me as if he had not heard.

– I can't sleep, I said.

He nodded.

– Perhaps, he said absently, you're meant to stay awake.

He flexed my right arm, studying the action of the joint.

– Much pain?

I didn't answer. He let go my arm, and leaned over my file and wrote in it, in his slow, meticulous hand.

– You can lead a normal life, he said. There is no reason not to.

He didn't look up. He had a way of speaking, toneless and dispassionate, as if he were alone, trying out the words just to see how they sounded.

– Give me a prescription, I said. Help me.

But he went on writing, slowly, carefully.

– I have helped you, he murmured.

Felix was not in the waiting room. I found him in the corridor, smoking. He asked me what the doctor had said, and when I told him he cackled, and threw his fag-end on the floor and trod on it. Then we went upstairs, and matron gave me a pocketful of pills. She looked at Felix in silence. He grinned. On the way out he said:

– That stuff, she just gives it to you, does she, no record of it or anything?

November rain in the streets, the traffic fuming and snorting. He liked to hear about the hours I had spent on the operating table, about the tinfoil bandages, the swabs and the scissors. He would wince, gritting his teeth and shutting one eye, waving his hands at me, pretending he wanted me to stop.

– But they brought you back to life, he said. And then you met up with me again. You see how things fall out? The Lord tempers the wind to the shorn lamb.

The lights were on at noon in the flat. Professor Kosok was pacing the cluttered front room. He wore black tubular trousers, boots with laces, a greasy bow-tie. He had an angry, waddling walk, his fat legs jerked, he twitched his arms, as if he were constricted at the groin, the armpits. He fixed me with his clouded small dark eyes. Adele sat in an armchair by the fireplace, wearing her plastic raincoat, leaning forward intently with her arms folded on her knees, staring at the single bar of the electric fire in the grate. There were dark shadows under her eyes. The fire had brought out a diamond pattern on her shins. An ashtray beside her on the floor was full.

– Well! said Felix happily, looking around at us and rubbing his hands. Here we are again!

Adele showed me places in the city I had never noticed, walled gardens in the midst of office blocks, odd-shaped little courtyards, an overgrown cemetery between a bakery and a bank. She walked quickly through the streets, canted forward a little, her sharp little face thrust out. Now and then she would stop and look about her searchingly, as if to verify something, some detail of the scene. She hardly spoke to me, glancing sidelong at my knees. We went into the big department stores and wandered along the brightly lit aisles, gazing in silence at the racks of gaudy clothes and toiletries and packaged foods as if they were artefacts in a museum, the works of an immemorial golden age. People stared at us, children tugged at their mothers' skirts and pointed, avid and agape. Adele took no notice. She lived in the city as if she were alone in it, as if it were somehow hers, a vast, windswept pleasure garden, deserted and decayed.

We dined in cheap cafés, sitting at plastic tables behind fogged windows, amid the smells of boiled tea and fried bread and fags. I watched the people around us, the raw-eyed lorry drivers, the dumpy girls with dyed blonde hair and laddered stockings, the gaunt, watchful young men in raincoats too small for them. They ate with a kind of dogged circumspection, crouching over their plates, their jaws working in a rhythmic, circular motion. They had a dull, shocked look about them, as if they were survivors of some enormous accident. Covertly I studied Adele too, her pinched, heart-shaped face, her chilblained hands. She hardly ate at all, but smoked without pause, drinking cups of thin, grey coffee. When she put the cigarette to her mouth she shut one eye, as if in pain, and drew in deeply, with a harsh little sigh. Sometimes she would talk, quietly, with intensity, her eyes fixed on the steamy window beside her. People followed her, she said, men stalked her at night through the streets, sat beside her on buses and touched her, murmuring things. A woman with red hair had come up behind her one day and cursed her, shrieking and spitting in her face. Then there were the tramps, the tinkers with their wild eyes, looking at her. A negro had stood behind her in a crowded shop and pressed himself against her.

– He had perfume on him, she said. The palms of his hands were pink.

Then she gave her high bird–cry of a laugh, and fixed me with that fraught, off-centre stare.

I showed her my old haunts, the alleys and archways, the streets by the river, the clay paths along the canal, where I had stalked the beggars and the madmen in those first, heady days of an autumn that now seemed an age ago. She grew restless, turning vaguely this way and that, as if she were looking for a way to escape. Sometimes still she would walk away from me abruptly, as on that first night on the quays, and jump on board a bus, or disappear down a sidestreet. She did it not from anger, or even rudeness, I think it was just that now and then my presence beside her somehow slipped her mind. I might not see her at all for days on end. I don't know where she went. She must have had a room somewhere. She insisted she did not live at the flat in Chandos Street, though she often stayed there, sleeping in one or other of the dingy back bedrooms. She kept her things there too, dispersed among the general clutter. There was a suitcase stuffed with clothes, which would make its way from the bedrooms through the front room to the hall, and then all the way back again. Everything shifted around like this, the professor's belongings too, the place always seemed as if a large untidy family had just moved in, or was about to move out. Adele picked her way through the jumble with her sleepwalker's frown, as if she had been looking for something and had forgotten what it was. One evening she showed me her syringe, a big old-fashioned thing with a calibrated glass barrel and a plunger with a steel thumb-hole. It had its own special box, like a jewel case, with a lid that snapped shut, and dark-blue velvet lining.

– He got it for me, she said.

We leaned over it, our foreheads almost touching, contemplating it in silence. Then she sighed and shut the lid on it, and took it with her out of the room. I stood at the big front window. The winter evening was drawing in. I could hear the distant blare of rush-hour traffic. The remains of one of her cigarettes smouldered in an ashtray on the mantelpiece. She never managed to extinguish the stubs completely, no matter with what force she crushed them out, her mouth working.

She was in the big, bare room at the back of the house. There was a narrow bed in a corner, a single dim bulb dangling from the ceiling. A gas fire hissed. The great windows were curtainless, looking out on a drab confusion of gardens. Night like a dark gas was seeping down on the city out of a luminous, mauve sky. She sat on the side of the bed, her head bowed, one hand hanging, the other resting palm upward across her knees. She had taken off her dress. One strap of her slip had fallen down her shoulder. She lifted her head when I came in, and cast about her vaguely, with a blank gaze. She ran a hand through her hair.

– I cut it all off, she said, one time. It grew back.

She blinked, frowning, and shook her head. Then she stood up, and drew the slip over her head and let it trickle through her fingers to the floor. Frail wrists, frail ankles, meagre flanks. Her delicate, glimmering shoulders. She had a plaster on one of her toes, where a chilblain had burst. She walked here and there about the room, shedding the rest of her things absent-mindedly as she went. She looked strange to me now, that known head on this unfamiliar, thin, almond-white body. There was a little triangular space between her legs, below the smudge of black hair. She lit a cigarette. When I touched her she turned quickly, startled. Her mouth was open, I kissed her clumsily, tasting smoke. She did not shut her eyes.

She turned off the light, and we lay down together on the narrow bed. She was trembling. Gradually the dim shapes of the room came forward out of the darkness, like creatures gathering silently around us. She clasped me tightly in her arms, yet at the same time seemed to hold me off from her, as if part of her attention were elsewhere, concentrating on something beyond me. The sheet was clammy. I was cold, and burning. My hands shook. I licked her eyelids, her armpits, I put my tongue into her ears, her navel, into the cool little cup at the base of her throat. When I made to delve in her lap, however, she drew away from me, and there was a sudden, frightening silence. Cautiously I tried again, but again she drew back. She would not be penetrated, at least not where I wanted most to penetrate her, and at last, with an impatient sigh, she turned away from me.

She lay on the edge of the bed, crouched and tense, staring away into the darkness like an animal listening, ready for danger. I held one of her cold, small breasts in my hand, my mouth was pressed to the nape of her neck. Her skin had a tawny, schoolgirl smell. I was shivering. The evening was still. The windows stared out into the darkness in blank amazement. An aeroplane flew over, its engines laboriously beating, I glimpsed its ruby wing-light sailing across the corner of the window above us. I was thinking of a moment from long ago, when I was a child, there was nothing in it, I don't know why I remembered it, just a moment on a bend on a hill road somewhere, at night, in winter, the wet road gleaming, and dead leaves spinning, and the light from a streetlamp shivering in the wind. Absence, I suppose, the forlorn weight of all that was not there, I suppose that's what I was remembering.

We dressed in silence. The gas fire sang its tiny song. My hands still trembled. Adele paced, frowning, from room to room, looking for something. She was hungry, she announced. We went out, and she bought a bag of chips and stood on the pavement outside the chip shop and devoured them, her eyes fixed in concentration on the ground before her, as if she were feeding not herself, but some starving thing inside her.

We went for a walk. It was a raw night, tempestuous and clear. A full moon dived and wallowed amid scudding clouds. We saw a fight outside a pub, and met a little woman pushing a little dog in a doll's pram. On a patch of waste ground a family of meths drinkers sat around a fire like a circle of decayed stone statues. We stood on a bridge and watched a barge slide past beneath us, dark and silent on the dark river. When we got back to Chandos Street the sick-looking young man was there, waiting on the corner, huddled in his coat against the wind, with his scrawny girl beside him. He attempted a sporty grin, his mouth twitching.

– Hello, chief, he said. Any stuff tonight? Listen, we're in a bad way, real sick.

I offered him a phial of Lemures. He snatched it from me, but when he read the label I thought he would weep.

– Not that, he said, that's no good. That other gear, you know? Like the last time?

He was sweating. The girl began to whimper. He turned and shouted at her to shut up, his voice cracking. Adele had walked on, with her head down.

– I haven't any, I said, backing away from him.

He came after me, rooting in the pockets of his coat, and brought out a wristwatch and thrust it under my nose.

– I'll give you this, he said. See, this? It's gold.

I put a hand in his chest and pushed him away. He stood, crestfallen, watching me retreat. He gave a sort of sob and stamped his foot.

– Christ, pal . . .

Adele was at the door. As I came up the steps she went inside and shut it quietly in my face.

FELIX WAYLAID ME one evening in the hall.
There was something he wanted to say to me, it was time
we had a talk. A door opened above us somewhere, he took
my arm and drew me hastily behind him down a gloomy
passageway beside the stairs. We stepped out into a yard.
There were dustbins, and a dank smell. He peered over his
shoulder cautiously, then winked at me, digging his
tremulous claws into my arm.

– Have to be careful, he said. He's always on the watch.
– Who?
He laughed.
– Who? Who do you think?
I followed him down the narrow garden. Everything
was overgrown with bindweed and briars. Tall skeletons of
last year's thistles stuck up starkly. The backs of houses rose
all around us. The sky was still light. A new moon was
visible above the chimney-pots. Felix put his hands in his
pockets and stopped to survey the scene.

– There is order in everything, he said. Isn't it wonderful?

Look at this place. It seems a wilderness, but underneath it all there's a garden.

He looked at me sidelong, smiling.

– What do you say?

I said:

– I don't know.

He took my arm again.

– Oh but you do, you do know, you of all people.

We walked along a weed-grown path, and came upon a dark pool overhung by a stunted, bare tree. Dim forms moved in the depths of the water. We stopped, and leaned to look, and slowly the fish floated up, like something in a dream, lifting weak, hopeful mouths, their pallid fins feebly beating the moss-brown water. Felix's face grinned up at me, with a fish-mouth for an eye.

– What are numbers, after all? he said. Music, that kind of thing, it's all sums, isn't it?

The bronze reflection of a cloud sailed on to the surface of the water, the arabian moon was there too, a horned sliver, glimmering. The fish sank again slowly, into the deeps.

– Come on, Felix said, let's go for a stroll. I have to see a man about a horse.

Dusk was settling in the streets, the lamps were coming on. There was a bitter wind, and patches of damp on the pavements. We walked by the railings of the square, under the dark trees. Felix pointed to the gutter.

– Ever wonder, he said, who it is removes squashed cats from the road? There was one run over there this morning, now it's gone.

He halted, cupping a hand to his ear. Music sounded faintly in the distance, a tinny blare.

– Hark! he said. The herald angels.

The office workers were going home, flitting like shadows through the brumous twilight, hurrying away to their unimaginable lives. We crossed the road, past great pillared arches and granite façades, and turned in the direction of the river. Two figures in long overcoats stood under a lamp-post, examining a bottle in a brown paper bag. Water was bubbling out of a crack in the paving where a pipe had burst. For an instant suddenly I saw into the dark heart of things, and a surge of mad glee rose in my gullet like waterbrash.

– The professor, now, Felix was saying. A hopeless case, I tell you, I've given him up for lost. Blind chance, he says, blind chance, that's all. As if chance was blind. We know better, don't we, Castor?

We passed under a railway bridge. An alleyway exhaled the sour stink of the river. The tide was high. We picked our way along the quay, over the slimed cobbles, and stopped by the side of a rusted cargo ship. The curved prow jutted above us, keen as an axe-blade. Felix peered up into the darkness and whistled softly. Running clouds were spilling past the rail up there like luminous smoke. He whistled again, and this time there was a faint answering note. A head appeared, and a hand waving, and presently two figures came down the gangway, hurrying silently on tiptoe. Felix started towards them, but paused and turned back to me.

– By the way, he said, the old boy wants you to work with him, did I mention it?

The sailors were hardy little men with bandy arms and legs. One wore a leather cap with a peak. His name was

Brand. He had a big pink face, and eyes set so close together they were almost one. He said nothing, only grinned, showing a mouthful of broken teeth. His companion was called Frisch. He had a high forehead and a prominent nose and hardly any chin.

– Dear friends . . . ! said Felix.

Frisch made a chopping gesture with the edge of his hand.

– *Ruhe!* he snarled. You want everyone to fokken hear?

We went to the Star of the Sea, a low, smoky dive with plastic seats, and yellowed prints of sailing ships on the walls. The bar was loud with merrymaking. We sat at a table in a corner, and Felix bought brandy for the sailors and sat and watched them drink, tapping his fingers on the table and smiling. Frisch, who seemed to regard everything with a profound, angry scepticism, buried his seal's snout in his glass and looked about him grimly at the weeping walls and the prints and the strings of coloured paper decorations. He eyed me too, and said to Felix:

– This is your tester, eh? Your *Chemiker*?

Felix laughed blandly.

– Oh no, he said, no. My . . . partner.

And he winked at me.

– *Ja*, Frisch said sourly, that is what he looks like.

They began to argue about money, or at least Frisch did, while Felix sat and smiled. Among the crowd at the bar someone fell over, and a cheer went up. Brand was peering about him out of his cyclop's eye with a kind of happy wonderment, lifting his leather cap and scratching his straw-coloured hair, as if he had never seen such a place before, with such jolly people in it. He drank another drink, and banged his glass on the table top and sang:

> Es war eine Ratt' im Kellernest,
> Lebte nur von Fett und Butter,
> Hatte sich ein Ränzlein angemäst't
> Als wie der Doktor Luther.

– Good man, Lars, Felix said. Sing up!

> Die Köchin hatt' ihr Gift gestellt,
> Da ward's so eng ihr in der Welt,
> Als hätte sie Lieb' im Leibe.

Then there were more drinks, and Frisch's rancorous mutterings grew slurred. Brand stood up, and put one foot up on the table and reached a lighted match between his legs and farted, igniting a brief blue spurt of flame. He sat down with a sheepish grin, rolling his shoulders bashfully, and pulled the peak of his cap over his eyes.
– Bravo, old firebrand! Felix said.
– *Arschloch*, Frisch mumbled, and curled his lip.
Brand grinned again, and ducked his head.
– Drink up! said Felix. Pip pip!
Frisch was growing increasingly angry, glaring about him unsteadily with a murderous eye and talking to himself. Brand began to sing again, but could not remember the words. His mood turned glum. Felix made a sign to me and rose, and after a moment I followed him. He was waiting for me in the street. He took my arm without a word and walked me around the side of the pub. In a

moment Frisch came out and stood looking up and down the quay, shouting drunkenly. Then Brand stumbled out, and took a gulp of night air, and immediately vomited on the pavement. Felix chuckled. We retreated down a lane.

– The people one has to do business with! Felix said.

The moon was high, a black wind scoured the streets. We arrived at a corner and found ourselves on the quay again. There was a broken blue wall, and a wooden fence, and a swollen woman drawn in chalk. We stopped under the street light.

– You see what fun you can have when you stick with me? Felix said. New friends, night rambles, interesting times. There's only one condition.

He was peering off into the darkness.

– That you don't, he said, lead a normal life.

And he laughed.

Two figures approached, going unsteadily, I thought it was Frisch and Brand, but it was not, it was the shaky young man from Chandos Street and his skinny girl. Felix went forward to meet them, taking something – something, that's rich! – from the deep inner pocket of his mackintosh. He and the young man spoke together briefly. The girl hung back. Then they went off again into the darkness, and Felix returned.

– As I say, he said. The people!

We walked along by the river, and crossed the bridge. There were not many abroad in that cold night. A group of youths stood in a shop doorway bawling out a carol. Chains of coloured lights were strung between the lamp-posts, dancing and rattling in the wind. Under the dark façade of a huge shabby office building Felix stopped and said:

– Well, here we are.

He laughed at my baffled look.

– I told you, he said. He wants you to work with him. I promised him you would. Now you won't let me down, will you?

He pointed to a flight of steps descending to a door in the basement of the building. He was smiling. Afar in the tempestuous night a peal of joybells sounded.

– Don't worry, he said. It's the season for beginnings, after all!

He skipped down the steps, his coat-tails flying, and pressed the doorbell with a flourish.

The door was opened by a plump young man in a yellow cardigan and suede slippers and a silk cravat. He had curls, and a broad soft sallow face, and a moist little mouth like the valve opening of a complicated inner organ. His name – let me have done with it – was Leitch. He looked at Felix with distaste and said:

– He's not here.

Felix only smiled at him, and after a moment's hesitation he shrugged and stepped back to let us pass. When I came forward into the light he laughed.

– Who's this? he said. The Phantom of the Opera?

Felix smiled again, with lips compressed, and wagged a finger at him in playful admonition. We were in a long, bare, clean corridor with white walls, and white rubber tiles on the floor. The air vibrated with a dense, soundless din that pressed upon the eardrums. We walked towards another door at the end of the corridor. Leitch padded behind us, I could feel his hostile eye. He was first at the door, though, skipping ahead of us on his slippered feet, like a corpulent ballet dancer, one plump hand pre-emptively lifted.

– Allow me, he said with a venomous trill.

The room was an immense, rectangular box with a low ceiling made of blocks of some white synthetic stuff. The floor here too was clad with white tiles. There were no windows. The machine was housed in big grey steel cabinets, they had about them a faint, pained air of startlement. They were so grand, so gracefully arranged, they might have been interrupted in the midst of a stately dance. For a moment even Felix hesitated on the threshold. This was their room. We were the wrong shape.

– Come in, Leitch said. Meet the monster.

He grinned scornfully, his pink mouth puckering, and started to walk away.

– Hang on, old chap, Felix said mildly. Aren't you going to show the new boy around?

Leitch looked from him to me and back again with deep dislike. It seemed he would refuse, but something in Felix's smile checked him. He shrugged, tugging angrily at his cravat.

– What does he want to see?

Felix laughed.

– Oh, everything! he said, and turned to me. Isn't that right? You want everything!

The machine was a Reizner 666. I had never seen

anything like it in my life, had not known such a thing could exist. Yet I recognized it. It hummed in the depths of its coils, dreaming its vast dream of numbers. It had a brain, a memory. I recognized it. Leitch showed me the rudiments of its workings. I hardly listened to him. The thing itself spoke to me, I touched its core and it quivered under my hand. When I pressed the keys on the console the print fell across the page with a soft crash. At my shoulder Felix chuckled.

– What a gadget, eh? he whispered.

Professor Kosok arrived, with his black coat and his hat and his badly furled umbrella. He stopped inside the door and stared at us. Then he took off his coat and threw it on a chair, and came and looked at the figures I had printed.

– What is this game? he said. This is not a toy.

It was Leitch he looked at. The young man scowled. Felix said:

– Well, I'll be off.

And with a wink he departed.

PROFESSOR KOSOK always worked by night. Often I had come upon him in the daytime in one of the bedrooms in Chandos Street, asleep on a bare mattress in a bundle of blankets and coats, only the top of his head and his nose showing. Now I too began to live a life at night, in that white room. The professor took scant notice of me. He existed in a constant state of angry preoccupation, stumping about in his waistcoat and his bow-tie, snorting softly to himself and rubbing a hand on his tussocky scalp. The machine was connected to others like it in other parts of the world, suddenly in the middle of the night the printer would spring to life of its own accord, rapping out peremptory, coded questions, like a medium's table. He would rush to the console and start excitedly to reply, but he could not work the keyboard properly, he kept making mistakes, to the growing annoyance of the machine, which would chatter and snap at him, and then retreat abruptly into a silent sulk, until Leitch, with a bored sneer, came and punched in the correct codes. Then, for hours, sheet after sheet of figures would fall into the wire tray, each one folding on to its fellows with an identical, silken sigh. When the transmission was finished Leitch and I would take the figures and sift through them for days, searching out intricate patterns of correspondence and repetition. Sometimes it was no more than a single repeating value that we hunted.

– Truffles, the professor would say, with a smile that twitched. And you are the pigs.

It was his one joke.

But he seemed to want only disconnected bits, oases of order in a desert of randomness. When I attempted to map out a general pattern he grew surly, and threw down his pencil on the console and stamped away, fuming. I turned to Leitch. He put on a pensive frown, pressing a finger to his forehead.

– We're searching for the meaning of life, he said.

And then laughed. He looked at me with contempt.

– How do I know what he's doing! he said. You're supposed to be the genius, you tell me. Statistics, probabilities, blind chance, I don't know. Why don't you ask him? He's half cracked, anyway.

But there was no asking anything of the professor, he would pretend he had not heard, and turn away, muttering.

Leitch's animosity was pure and disinterested. He directed it equally at all who came near him. It was like a task that had been assigned to him, irksome, and thankless, from which he was not allowed to relax. His name was Basil. He suffered from attacks of breathlessness, which he tried to hide from me. His feet were bad too, something was wrong with the arches, he walked in his slippers with a rolling gait, the voluminous seat of his trousers sagging. He had a painful, polished look that spoke of long sessions in the bathroom, of dousings and dustings, and ashen gloomings into a cruel mirror. He wore a gold chain on his wrist, and a ring with two gold hands holding a gold heart. He consoled himself with food. He ate alone, a lugubrious sybarite, sitting in a far corner of the room with a plastic bag open in his lap and a paper napkin tucked under his cravat. He had sandwiches, meat pies, cakes, cold chicken legs. I pictured him, bent at a table in a greasy room somewhere, some other Chandos Street, slicing and buttering, as the light faded on another solitary winter afternoon. Yet there was something almost impressive in his intransigence and grim self-sufficiency. Sucking at a bruised peach, or gobbling a fistful of purple grapes, he had the air of a ruined emperor, with those curls, that great pallid face, those wounded, unforgiving eyes.

– Just do your job, will you? he said. Just do your job, and leave me alone.

I had hardly spoken a word to him all night.

– What job? I said. Is this a job?

He turned to me with blood in his eye.

– You're here, aren't you? he snarled. What more do you want?

Nothing, I wanted nothing, I was almost happy there. How calm the nights were, with only the hum of the machine, and the professor's soft mutterings, and all around us the darkness. We might have been a mile under the ocean. We saw no one. We lived in downtime. The machine's real users were those who came here during the day, from the offices above. I wondered about them, and searched for their traces. Sometimes there would be a coffee cup left behind, or an ashtray in which a half-smoked cigarette had burned itself out, leaving a fragile fossil of ash and a smear of tar. One night I arrived and found a yellow cardigan draped on the back of a chair, where someone had forgotten it. We did not move it, even Leitch avoided touching it, and as the night wore on it became a more and more insistent, numinous presence, unsettling as a pair of golden wings.

The machine was a presence too, a great tame patient beast, tethered in its white cage. It had its voices, the faint flutter and tick of the memory bank scanning, the printer's crash and clatter. One of the storage discs produced an unaccountable, piercing shriek when it was first switched on. And always there was that dense hum, that made the very air vibrate. Sometimes, in the early hours, when one or other of my limbs began to sing, like a burning stick singing in a fire, I would seem to hear a sort of chime, like a small, sustained chord, as if the machine's voice and the voice of my pain had found a common note. When something went wrong we were supposed to call for an engineer, but we never did. Instead, Leitch would get out his forceps and his probes and delve into the delicate innards of the machine, past the lattice of switches and bundles of wires fine as hair, down into the secret core itself. Then for a moment, forgetting himself, he would be transformed, kneeling there in the midst of that white light, absorbed, intent, like an attendant figure in the foreground of a luminous nativity. He talked to the machine in a fierce undertone, cursing and cajoling it. Always it gave in. He would sit back on his heels then, grey sweat on his forehead and his upper lip, wiping his hands, his fat shoulders drooping and his eyes going dead.

I brought in the black notebook, and in idle hours went over again the old, insoluble problems, playing them over, move by move, like drawn grandmaster games. Infinity was still infinity, zero still gaped, voracious as ever. The professor stopped behind me, and peered over my shoulder.

– Pah, he said. Antique stuff. History.

At dawn, without a word, the three of us went our separate ways, the professor bundled in his black coat, Leitch with his empty foodbag under his arm, and I behind them, dawdling. I liked to walk the streets at that early hour. The wind rustled over pavements hard and grey as bone, and gulls scavenged in the gutters. Traffic lights blossomed from green to red and back again, silent as flowers. A solitary motor car would pass me by, the driver propped like a manikin behind a windscreen flowing with reflections of a cold grey sky and paper-coloured clouds. Sometimes I went to Chandos Street, in hope that Adele would be there. Instead I would often find the professor, sitting at the table by the big window in the kitchen, still in his coat and hat, gazing out at the street, a mug of tea going cold at his elbow. These encounters were faintly, inexplicably embarrassing.

Adele never asked where I went at night, as I never asked where she was when she disappeared for days on end.

I think when I was away from her she forgot about me. Oh, I don't mean forgot, exactly, but that she lost hold of something, some essential of the fact of my existence. For that is how it was with me, when she was not there, something of her faded in my mind, she became transparent. Even when she was in my arms she was also somehow absent. I never had, not for an instant, her entire attention. Perhaps it is as well. It occurs to me I might not have survived the full force of her presence. What does that mean? I don't know, I don't know – there's so much darkness here. She regarded my injuries as if they were not part of me, as if they were something that had attached itself to me, like a stray dog. She would raise herself on an elbow and study me, touching my withered arm, or running a finger over the knots and whorls of my chest, frowning to herself. What was she thinking? I never asked. She would not have answered. One day she said:

– Did you think you were going to die, when it happened?

She was sitting up in bed, with a blanket around her shoulders, and an ashtray on the mattress beside her. The day outside was bitter under a louse-grey sky, down in the garden the bare trees shuddered. I think of that moment, and I'm there again.

– Something inside me is wearing out, she said. Some part, wearing out.

I had met her in the hall. She was in fur boots and a beret, and a moth-eaten fur coat. Her mood was frenetic she fixed her icy fingers on my wrist and laughed, and a bubble of saliva came out of her mouth and burst. Upstairs

I took her coat. Slivers of the cold air of outdoors fell like silverfish from its folds. In bed she held my sex in her chill hand and laughed and laughed, throwing back her head and offering me her throat to feed on. She would not let me inside her, shut her legs. I clutched her against me, muttering and moaning, and at last, to placate me, she knelt impatiently and put her head in my lap, and I spilled myself in a series of voluptuous slow shivers into the hot wet hollow of her mouth. Her arm lay across my chest, with its track of puncture marks running from wrist to elbow, like the stippled scar of a briar scratch, and I thought of childhood.

Felix was in the front room, lounging on the horsehair sofa reading a newspaper.

– Ah, there you are, Grendel, he said. How are you? Sit down, talk to me. We haven't seen each other for a while, you've been neglecting your old friends.

I sat down at the table. A pigeon landed on the sill outside and looked in, the wind ruffling its neck feathers. Felix tossed the paper aside and leaned forward with his hands pressed between his knees. He was wearing his mac, and a flat cap pushed back on his head. There were shallow indents at his temples, I had never noticed them before. Sometimes when I looked at him closely like this he seemed a stranger.

– How goes the great work? he said. Is the prof treating you right? And what about the fat boy, does he stick to you, hey?

Adele came from the bedroom, barefoot, in her fur coat. Seeing him there she paused, then came to the table and searched in her bag for a cigarette with one hand, holding her coat shut with the other. He grinned at her, bending low to look up into her face. She said:

– How did you get in here?

– Ah, he said. Good question.

He went on grinning. There was silence. Adele smoked, frowning vaguely, her eyes fixed on the table. Felix looked from her to me, and then at her again. He chuckled.

– Having fun, you two, are you? he said. Fun and games, yes?

The pigeon flew from the sill with a clatter of wings. Felix leaned back on the sofa, one ankle crossed on a knee, and fished out his tobacco tin.

I said:

– Why did you say that he wanted me to work for him?

He lit up a butt, and blew two thick cones of smoke from his pinched nostrils. He looked at me narrowly and smiled.

– Because he did, he said. Why else?

– He doesn't say a word to me.

– Ah, but that's his way, you see.

Adele went and sat in front of the electric fire, holding up one bare foot and then the other to the heat. The last wan light of day was fading in the window.

– It's true, Felix said, I may have exaggerated a little. But I didn't say he *said* it, did I? I only said he wanted you, and that's different.

He rose and walked to the window, and stood there with his back to the room, looking out into the winter twilight.

– People don't recognize what it is they want, he said. They have to be shown. I have to . . . interpret.

He glanced at me merrily over his shoulder.

– Oh, yes, Pinocchio, he said. By jiminy, yes.

Adele suddenly laughed, one of her brief, high shrieks, and threw her cigarette into the grate and lit another. Then she put a hand to her forehead and bowed her head. Felix was smiling back at me still. Darkness advanced into the room.

I ONLY WENT TO the hospital now when I needed a new supply of pills. I avoided Dr Cranitch. Matron looked at me with her sad eyes, saying nothing. I gave all my attention to the notices on the walls in the dispensary while she filled up the little mauve phials for me. She put a fresh wad of cotton wool in each one, and wrote out new labels in her neat, schoolgirl's hand. Miss Barr was asking after me, she said, Father Plomer too. She did not look up. Through the window behind her I could see down into the grounds. A wash of sunlight fell across the grass and was immediately extinguished. An old man on a crutch was hobbling up the drive. I picked up the pills. She watched my hands, and then she turned away.

At the gates a car pulled up and Felix stuck out his head and hailed me.

– What a lucky chance, he said. Hop in, we're going to a party.

The car was a shuddering, ramshackle machine, coughing

and farting in a cloud of blue exhaust smoke. The young man with the shakes was at the wheel. His girl sat behind him in the back seat, huddled against the window. It was starting to rain.

– Come on, Felix said to me, don't be a spoilsport.

The young man's name was Tony. When I got in he turned and winked at me.

– Hiya, pal, he said.

There were livid bags under his eyes.

We crossed the river. Gusts of wind were smacking the steel-blue water, and pedestrians on the bridge walked at an angle, their coat-tails whipping.

– There are these people, Felix was saying, we're to meet them at the Goat . . .

Tony laughed, a high-pitched whinny.

– The Goat! he cried.

The girl shrank away from me, staring out the window beside her with a fist pressed to her mouth. She had a blank white face and frightened eyes and a tiny, pink-tipped nose. Her name was Liz. Big drops of rain swept against the windscreen.

– Fucking wipers, Tony said.

Then abruptly the rain stopped, and there was sun. We drove along by the canal. The poplars were still bare. Great bundles of cloud were sailing across a porcelain sky. Felix turned around in his seat to face me.

– Seeing the lady in white, were you? he said. Wangling bonbons out of her again? Let's have a look.

He held the little bottle of Lamias aloft between a finger and thumb, squinting at it as if it were a rare vintage, and shook his head in laughing wonderment.

– Do you know what these things are worth? he said. Do you?

– They're gold, pal, Tony said, nodding at me in the driving mirror. Pure gold.

He wanted to take one. Felix laughed.

– Anthony, is that wise?

– Fuck wise, said Tony.

Beside me Liz was rolling a cigarette in a little machine. Twice she had to stop and start all over again. Then she spilled a box of matches on the seat. For a moment it seemed she would cry. I tried to help her gather up the matches, but when I put out a hand towards her she flinched in fright and went suddenly still, averting her face from me, her little pink nose twitching.

We were heading towards the mountains.

Tony was bouncing in his seat, beating a tattoo with the flat of his hand on the steering wheel.

– Whoo! he said. That stuff!

He looked at me in the mirror again, his eyes wide and shining bright.

– Gold! he said, and the wheel wobbled.

– Calm yourself! cried Felix, laughing. We'll all be killed.

We left the city behind, and climbed a long hill, the old car groaning, then crossed a bare brown plateau. Sunlight and shadow swept the far peaks. Sheep fled into the ditches at our approach. Tony was crooning quietly to himself.

– Ah, how good it is to get into the open, Felix said. The mountains, the mountains, I've always felt at home in the mountains.

We descended a winding road and stopped at a little oasis of wind-racked pines. There was an ancient pub with fly-blown windows, and an antique petrol pump in front of the door. Chickens scratched about on a patch of oil-stained gravel, among a dozen or more parked cars. I stepped out into the cold, sharp air. Water was running over stones somewhere close by. A flush of wind shook the pines, and all at once it was spring.

The pub was dim inside. A wireless muttered somewhere. Vague figures inhabited the gloom, they eyed us cautiously as we entered. A fat man in a dirty apron emerged from a door behind the bar, chewing. He wiped his mouth on his apron, and put his big hands on the counter and loomed at us with an expression of mingled servility and craft. Felix grandly smiled.

– Dan, my friend . . .

I was looking at the other customers, gathered there behind us like shades, watching us. They too had come here from the city. They had something about them I seemed to recognize. There were girls who looked like Liz, and ragged young men like Tony, but that was not it. I thought of my time in the hospital, the hours I had spent among the brotherhood of the maimed. That dulled, neuralgic air of waiting, suspended. That silence. They shuffled closer. Felix turned and surveyed them, smiling, one heel hooked on the foot-rail and his elbows planted on the bar.

– Look at them, he said in my ear. They know the doctor's arrived.

Tony went off to the lavatory. Others followed, in ones and twos. He did not come back for a long time. The afternoon was ending, the setting sun glared redly in the window, then faded. Liz sat on a bar-stool, drinking glasses of stout. She smoked and coughed. I caught her watching me. This time she did not look away. She asked for one of my pills. When I took out the phial Felix put a hand hastily over mine, looking about us sharply.

– That's gold, remember, he said with a smile, and this is Outlaw Gulch.

A sort of groggy gaiety began to spread. Two young men linked arms and danced a spidery jig. A girl laughed and laughed. Dan the barman stood behind his cash register and watched with a worried eye the traffic coming and going in the passageway out to the lav. Felix sighed happily and softly sang:

O God, how vain are all our frail delights . . .

Then Tony came back with his hands stuck in the pockets of his tight trousers, grinning and twitching.

– Surgery over? Felix said. Everybody cured?

– Except me, Tony said.

The twitching had spread from his jaw into his arms, now one of his legs began to shake. Liz was pawing at his sleeve.

– He gave me, she said, giggling, he gave me one of . . .

He flung her hand away.

– Get off me! he shrieked. Jesus.

He was sweating. He looked into Felix's face imploringly, with a broken smile. Felix laughed and turned to me.

– The doctor is sick, I think, he said.

– Come on, Tony whispered, gritting his teeth. Come on, don't . . .

Felix turned back to him blandly.

1 8 2

– But Anthony, tell me, who'll drive us home, if you get well?

The two young men who had been dancing had fallen down now, and lay on their backs waving their arms and legs feebly in the air. One of them seemed to be weeping. Tony put a hand to his forehead. Liz was watching him with a sort of glazed curiosity.

– I'll be all right, he said. Honest, I'll be . . .

Felix waved a hand.

– Oh, go on, then, he said, heal thyself.

Tony carried himself off to the lavatory, plunging sideways through the dimly milling crowd. A fight had broken out, there were screams and curses, and Dan lumbered from behind the bar, bellowing. A girl with a bleeding eye fell headlong on the floor. Someone kept laughing. Liz got down from the stool with a thoughtful, ashen look.

– Oh, she said, I think I'm going to spew.

Then suddenly I was outside in the cold black glossy night, under an amazement of stars. I could smell the pines, and hear the wind rushing in their branches. My head swam. Something surged within me, yearning outwards into the darkness. And all at once I saw again clearly the secret I had lost sight of for so long, that chaos is nothing but an infinite number of ordered things. Wind, those stars, that water falling on stones, all the shifting, ramshackle world could be solved. I stumbled forward in the dark, my arms extended in a blind embrace. On the gravel by the petrol pump a woman squatted, pissing. The fight was still going on somewhere, I could hear cries and groans. Felix rose up in front of me with a dark laugh.

– Creatures of the night! he said. What music they make!

We climbed the winding road to the crest of the hill. From here we could see afar the glittering lights of the city. The wind drummed above us, beating through the hollows of the air.

– Consider! Felix said in a loud voice, as if addressing a multitude. Is it not meet, is it not worthy, this world?

A pared moon had risen, by its faint light I could see his smile. He took my arm.

– Haven't I taken you places, though, he said. Eh? And shown you things. Blessed are the freaks, for they shall inherit the earth.

Tony came up the hill in the car then, crouching haggard-eyed over the wheel. Liz was slumped asleep in the back. Felix got in, but I lingered on the dark road, drunk on the knowledge of the secret order of things. The wind swirled, the stars trembled. I seemed to fall upwards, into the night.

E V E R Y T H I N G H A D brought me to this knowledge, there was no smallest event that had not been part
of the plot. Or perhaps I should say: had brought me
back to it. For had I not always known, after all? From the
start the world had been for me an immense formula. Press
hard enough upon anything, a cloud, a fall of light, a cry in
the street, and it would unfurl its secret, intricate equations.
But what v. as different now was that it was no longer
numbers that lay at the heart of things. Numbers, I saw at
last, were only a method, a way of doing. The thing itself
would be more subtle, more certain, even, than the mere
manner of its finding. And I would find it, of that I had no
doubt, even if I did not as yet know how. It would be a
matter, I thought, of waiting. Something had opened up
inside me on the mountain, some rapt, patient, infinitely
attentive thing, like a dark flower opening its throat to the
right. Now, as spring quickened around me, the city came
alive, like a garden indeed, flushed and rustling, impatient
and panting, with vague shrills and swoopings on all sides

in the lambent, watercolour air. I put aside the black notebook, it annoyed me now, with its parade of contradictions and petty paradoxes, its niggling insinuations. Why should I worry about the nature of irrational numbers, or addle my brain any longer with the puzzle of what in reality a negative quantity could possibly be? Zero is absence. Infinity is where impossibilities occur. Such definitions would suffice. Why not? I went out into the streets, I walked and walked. It was here, in the big world, that I would meet what I was waiting for, that perfectly simple, ravishing, unchallengeable formula in the light of which the mask of mere contingency would melt. At times it felt as if the thing would burst out into being by its own force. And with it surely would come something else, that dead half of me I had hauled around always at my side would somehow tremble into life, and I would be made whole, I don't know how, I don't know, but I believed it, I wanted to believe it. The feeling was so strong I began to think I was being followed, as if really some flickering presence had materialized behind me. I would stop in the street and turn quickly, and at once everything would assume a studied air of innocence, the shopfronts and façades of houses looking suspiciously flat and insubstantial, like a hastily erected stage-set. More than once I was convinced I had seen a shadow of movement, the fading after-image of a figure darting into a doorway, or skipping behind the trunk of a tree. Then for a second, before I had time to tell myself I had imagined it, I sensed with a shiver the outlines of another, darker, more dangerous world intermingled invisibly with this one of sky and green leaves and faded brick.

Everything must change. What had I ever done but drift? Now at last I would have purpose, order. Felix approved.

– That's it, he said, be positive. What did I tell you? I knew we were alike all along.

Suddenly I had seen the error I had been making. I had mistaken pluralities for unities. For the world is like numbers, the things that happen in it are never so small they cannot be resolved into smaller things. How could I have lost sight of that? I rummaged through the recent past, looking for the patterns that I must have missed. But, as once with numbers, so now with events, when I dismantled them they became not simplified, but scattered, and the more I knew, the less I seemed to understand.

I threw myself into work at the white room with a new passion. What more likely place for the light of certainty to dawn? The professor flew into one of his sudden fits of irritation.

– What is exact in numbers, he said, except their own exactitude?

– No, I said, no, not the numbers themselves, but . . .

He folded his stubby arms and glared at me like a vexed owl. His right eye-socket was larger than the left, it always made him look as if he were wearing a monocle.

– Well? he said. What, tell me.

– I don't know, I said. Something else.

He snorted.

– What else is there, but numbers?

The printer sprang into clattering life, he turned to it with a scowl. Leitch looked at me sidelong and sneered, slipping a piece of chocolate into that little pink prehensile mouth.

That was the night Miss Hackett came to see us. She was a thin tall woman of middle age with a prominent sharp face and lacquered brass hair. She put her head around the door that led from the offices upstairs, with a smile that was at once both arch and roguish. Leitch, slumped at the console, sat upright hastily and stared at her. She came in and shut the door behind her and advanced on him purposefully, with a hand thrust out, still playfully smiling, her lips compressed, as if we were children and she had slipped into the nursery to bring us a treat. She wore a tweed business suit and a white blouse with ruffles at the throat. She had a mannish walk, her high heels coming down briskly on the floor in a series of sharp, smart blows. Leitch got to his feet, stuffing the empty wrapper from the chocolate bar into his pocket with surreptitious haste. She stopped in front of him with a snap.

– Mr Cossack, she said brilliantly. I'm Hackett. So pleased.

There was a smear of lipstick on one of her large front teeth. Leitch tittered in fright and put his hands behind his back.

– Oh! he said. No, I'm not . . .

A tiny flaw appeared in Miss Hackett's smile, like a hairline crack in a china cup. She cast a questing glance about her. She had already taken me in, without quite looking directly at me. Professor Kosok came in from the lavatory in the corridor, still fumbling with his flies. For a moment he did not notice her. She waited, beaming, as he shuffled forward. When at last he saw her he stopped short, rearing back a little, his wide eye growing wider. She seized his hand and shook it violently once, as if she were cracking a whip. She seemed to think he must be deaf, for when she spoke she shouted.

– Hackett! she said. Thought I'd just pop in and say hello!

He continued to regard her with a grim surmise. She heaved a brisk little sigh and glanced about her brightly.

– Well! she said. And how goes the good work?

Leitch and I looked at each other, and immediately a truce was tacitly agreed between us. In the face of all the possible things Miss Hackett might represent, even Leitch felt in need of an ally. She carried a briefcase under her arm, a wafer-slim pouch made of burnished soft leather, it bespoke a marvellous importance. She fixed on the console, pointing a finger tipped with gules.

– This must be the nerve centre, I suppose? she said. It looks so complicated!

There was a brief silence. The professor grunted, and turned his back, motioning at Leitch with a cursory wave to show her the machine. Leitch put on a sickly smile and cleared his throat. Before he could speak, however, Miss Hackett held up a hand to silence him.

– Yes, thank you, she said quickly, with a sort of steely graciousness. I'm afraid I'm a feather-head when it comes to these contraptions.

The professor was poring over the printer. He was in his waistcoat and shirt-sleeves, the tabs of his braces on show. With her head on one side she considered him, taking aim at him between the shoulder-blades.

– I'm just here for a chat, she murmured. Just a chat.

She went and stood at the printer, and for a moment both of them watched in silence the sheets of figures coming up.

– How fast it goes! she said, leaning to look more closely.

And so much of it! You know, we've been so impressed with the quantity of the material you produce here.

Professor Kosok grunted again, and again walked away from her. She continued to watch the print-out, shaking her head in a little show of admiring wonderment. The professor sat down at the console, breathing hard, and started to stab at the keys with two stiff index fingers, like an amateur pianist in a temper. Leitch and I stood on either side of him. Miss Hackett came and hovered at his shoulder. It was like a little recital, we might have been gathered around the parlour piano.

– Of course, Miss Hackett said with a silvery laugh, we have noticed a certain lack of . . . well, of results, shall we say?

She waited, but he went on hitting the keys as if he had not heard. She took a deep breath, and grasping my arm she moved me firmly aside, and executed a swift little twirl that brought her to a half-sitting position against the console, facing him, with her arms folded and her ankles neatly crossed. She flashed her nursery smile again, and inclined her head and peered into his face, twinkling at him.

– The minister, you know, she said in a playfully menacing tone, the minister likes results.

He lifted his hands at last violently from the keyboard, and turned around in his chair and looked up at Leitch with a harsh laugh.

– Results! he said. She wants results!

He turned again and glared at her.

– What are you talking about? he said. What do you mean, what results are these, that this minister expects?

She pounced, leaning forward with sudden force and bringing her hands together in a soundless clap.

– But that's the point! she cried gaily. That's what we want you to tell us! You see?

Leitch, for some reason, laughed.

She rose from her perch on the console, tucking her briefcase more firmly under her arm, and stepped past me. She was careful not to touch me this time, no doubt recalling, more vividly than she would have wished, the feel of that stick-like thing inside my sleeve. She walked off a little way, head bowed in thought, then turned and retraced her steps slowly.

– We are all aware, she said, what an honour it is that you are working here, a person of your . . . your . . . And of course, in such a case the cost is not a large consideration.

– Cost, what cost? the professor cried. This is night-time.

Leitch coughed.

– Downtime, he said softly.

The professor turned in his chair again and glared at him. Miss Hackett waved away these interruptions, frowning, making a great show of following her train of thought.

– But we have our masters, you see, she said, even the minister is accountable.

She stopped in front of him, smiling down at him pensively, letting her gaze wander over his irate brow and pop eye, his clenched jaw with its ginger bristles, his bow-tie, his boots. Then in a flash she had drawn up a chair and plumped down on it, pressing her briefcase firmly on her knees, with an air of setting all constraints aside and getting down finally to the real business.

– My dear sir, she said. Listen. When you came to us first you spoke of conducting certain studies. I have the documentation here.

She gave the briefcase a friendly smack, as if it were the head of a trusty hound.

– It's vague, she said. The documents are vague. We were vague, at the time. You, forgive me, were vaguest of all.

The professor stood up abruptly and stamped away from her, rubbing a hand over his scalp, his short legs working angrily.

– Studies, yes! he said. I am conducting studies! You think I lied?

Miss Hackett shook her head, still blandly smiling.

– No no no, she said soothingly, with pursed lips. What an idea! Of course there is no question of . . . fraud. Only, this machine, you see, it costs such a lot of money to run, even in . . .

She looked to Leitch, who breathed, fawning.

– Downtime, he said.

She thanked him with an almost coquettish little bob of her head, her brazen waves tossing.

– Cost! the professor said. Pah!

Miss Hackett with a deft glance consulted her watch, then drew a breath and tried again. She spoke in a soft voice, slowly, giving a pert, interrogative flick to the ends of her sentences.

– We're only asking, she said, the minister is only asking, for some sort of statement of your precise aims in this programme? Everything you show us seems so . . . well, so hazy, so . . . uncertain?

192

At this the professor made a violent whooshing noise, like a breathless swimmer breaking the surface, and turned on her in a fury.

– There is no certainty! he cried. That is the result! Why don't you understand that, you you you . . .! Ach, I am surrounded by fools and children. Where do you think you are living, eh? This is the world, look around you, look at it! You want certainty, order, all that? Then invent it!

He flung himself down on his chair, fuming, twisting his head from side to side and yanking at his bow-tie, his legs furiously twitching. There was a silence. Miss Hackett gave a delicate cough and touched a hand to her hair. She glanced at Leitch, at me, even, with a brittle, brave little smile, to show us how patient she was, how dauntless, then she considered the professor again, chidingly, as if he were a big, recalcitrant baba.

– I'm sure I didn't mean to make you angry, she said. I only came to have a friendly chat. The minister wanted to send someone else, but I said no, no need for that, yet. Let me go, I said, he'll talk to me. After all, I am a statistician, in a manner of speaking.

The professor waved a weary dismissive hand.

– Oh, statistics . . .! he murmured, shaking his head.

– But I see, Miss Hackett went on, I see I was mistaken. In fact, I've wasted my time, haven't I. And now it's late, and I must leave you.

She stood up, smoothing her skirt, and tucked her briefcase under her arm. Leitch wallowed forward, for a second it seemed he might pick her up and carry her, in apology and reverence, to the door. Suddenly the professor gave another of his brief harsh laughs, and rose and pushed his face up into hers, pointing a finger at me.

– There! he said. Him! He is the one you need, he thinks that numbers are exact, and rigorous, tell your minister about him!

They turned, all three, and gazed at me for a moment in silence. Miss Hackett frowned. The professor shook his head again.

– And look at him, he said. Just look.

They might have been standing on the edge of a hole, peering in. Then Miss Hackett roused herself, and summoned up a last, steely smile.

– Well, she said to the professor, goodnight, no doubt you will be hearing from us, in due course.

Halfway to the door she halted, Leitch shambling at her heels almost collided with her. She looked about the room, wrinkling her nose, as if she were noticing the place for the first time. The printer nattered, the air hummed.

– What a dungeon this is, she said. How you can stand it . . .!

When she was gone Leitch looked at the professor with a vengeful eye.

– You've done it now, he said. Oh, you've done it now, all right.

Things were never to be the same again between Leitch and me after that night. It was as if we had been caught up together in some desperate, accidental drama, and the shared danger had forced on us an intimacy as awkward as it was inescapable. He became talkative. He complained about the professor, called him an old fucker, told me of other enormities he had committed before that night. He sat hunched over the console, fat and venomous, muttering. Somehow Miss Hackett's visit had lanced the boil of his bitterness, now the poison all came pouring out. He had not been treated right, he had never been treated right. They were all against him, people, all against him, just because – but there he broke off, and cast at me a narrow, distrustful look. His eyes were haunted, sunk in their pools of violet shadow, turbid, and somehow sticky, like two brown water-snails. He talked about Miss Hackett too, softly, in a sort of reverie of disgust. He made up jokes in which she suffered the most intricate indecencies. His knowledge of female anatomy was impressive, Felix called him a spoiled gynaecologist. He would put a warm hand on my wrist, chuckling, and lean his head at my ear and whisper another good one. I could never manage more than a wan smile in response, but it did not matter, he hardly noticed, he only wanted to hear himself saying the words. When Felix was there, though, he kept silent. Felix watched him, delighted with him, his slippers and his cravat, his bloated belly, that wary, aquatic eye.

– I say, Basil, he would say, what's a gay blade like you doing in this queer hole, eh?

And he would wink at me, with an artful smile, and put up his feet on the console and light a butt from his box.

We waited for what would follow Miss Hackett. Leitch expected the worst, though he never said exactly what he thought the worst would be. One night the telephone rang, until then I had not even noticed it was there. Professor

Kosok answered it, and stood and listened to its tiny, irate voice for a long time, pulling at his lower lip and scowling. He said little, and at last slammed down the receiver. When it rang again he left it off the hook. Then the volume of transmissions began to slacken, it was hardly noticeable at first. Sometimes the printer would stop abruptly, in the middle of a line of figures, and sit in silence for minutes on end, with an uncanny air of smugness and knowing. Leitch insisted he could find no fault, that they must have stopped sending at the other end, and the professor would shout at him, until at last the printer started up again, as if nothing had happened. The day-people were staying later and later, once when I arrived they were just leaving, I spotted a hand closing the door, and heard them laughing on the stairs. The seats of the chairs were still warm.

Felix dropped in at all hours, arriving sometimes in the early morning, when we were finishing. He always looked as if he had been up all night, doing things. He and I would go out together into the dawn, and walk along by the grey river, in the mist. I remember those mornings with peculiar clarity, the silence over the city, the gulls wheeling, the pale spring sunlight struggling through the grime, that particular shade of lavender in the dense air above the rooftops. He talked about the professor, asked in an offhand way about the work we were doing. I think he thought I was keeping things from him, he would give me a long look, quizzically smiling, his head thrown back and one rufous eyebrow arched. I told him about Miss Hackett, and he laughed.

– So they're on to him, eh? he said. Better take care, Philemon, that you don't get washed away along with him.

IT WAS ON ONE OF those mornings with Felix that – no, he wasn't there, it was just a morning, in April. The professor was away too, I don't know where, it doesn't matter. The flat was silent. There was the remains of a meal on the table in the front room, and a brimming ashtray. I stood at the window, not wanting to leave, not wanting to stay either. Pain had started up its thrumming tune, as it did at this weary hour every morning, I imagined something inside me, all knees and terrible elbows, plucking at my nerves. The street was deserted. In one of the houses opposite I could faintly hear a telephone ringing, it went on and on. The silence congregated at my back, it was like some large mute beast, nudging at me gently, with a kind of mournful insistence. I did not like to be alone like that, in a room not my own, I felt as if I were a stranger, I mean a stranger to myself, as if there were two of us, I and that other, that interloper standing up inside me, sharing in secret this pillar of frail flesh and pain. But then, I was not alone.

She was in the dingy bathroom on the landing, I found

her when I tried to open the door and something was
stopping it. She lay in a huddle with her knees drawn up to
her chest and one bare arm flung out. She was wearing her
plastic raincoat over her slip. One of her bare feet was
wedged against the door, I had to hold my breath and
squeeze sideways through the opening. When I knelt beside
her she stirred and gave a fluttering, vaguely protesting
sigh, like a sleeping child unwilling to be wakened from a
dream. Her hands were icy, she must have been lying here
for hours. There was a blue bruise turning yellow in the
hollow of her elbow.

– Adele, I said. Adele.

It sounded foolish.

I gathered her up in my arms. She had wet herself. She
was unexpectedly heavy, a chill, clammy limpness that I
could hardly hold. Her raincoat squeaked and crackled
when I lifted her. I got my foot around the door to open it,
but lost my balance and swayed off to one side, like a
caracoling horseman, and for a moment I was trapped
there, with one foot in the air and my shoulder pressed to
the wall. A tap was dripping in the handbasin. The window
behind the lavatory was open, down in the garden a
blackbird piped a repeated, liquid note, that too was like
water dripping. When I turned my head a magnified eye,
my own, loomed at me in a shaving mirror. I looked at
things around me, that tap, an old razor, a mug with a
toothbrush standing in it, their textures blurred and
thickened in the ivory light of morning, and I felt for a
second I was being shown something, it flashed out at me
slyly and then was gone, like a coin disappearing in a
conjuror's palm.

I got her to the front room and put her on the sofa, propped against the armrest. Her head kept slipping down. I must have stood there for a long time, transfixed, just looking at her. Then I strode into the kitchen and back again, to the bedrooms, wringing my hands, looking for I don't know what. I brought her ragged fur coat and wrapped it around her. I think I was talking to her all the while, I recall dimly the dull blare of a voice in the background, cajoling and hectoring, it can only have been mine. I recall too the Parisian delicacy of the spring morning, with faint traffic sounds and the clatter of pigeons, a puff of white cloud in the corner of the window, that big pale parallelogram of sunlight on the floor at my feet.

Then the ambulance arrived, and a curious, dreamy lentor took hold of everything. I suppose I expected a great commotion, sirens and the screech of brakes, boots on the stairs, shouts. Instead there was a polite ring on the bell, and two cheerful, burly men in uniform came in, carrying a rolled-up stretcher. They had an air of having known exactly what they would find. They went to work calmly, one wrapping Adele in a red blanket while the other unrolled the stretcher. Then together they lifted her deftly from the sofa, and fastened a leather strap across her shoulders and another across her knees, and one of them leaned down and brushed a damp strand of hair from her cheek. She was so pale, so peaceful now, like an effigy of a martyred child. Down in the street the radio in the ambulance muttered at intervals. They set the stretcher on the pavement while they got the back doors open. Adele woke up and looked about her wildly. She clutched my sleeve.

– What have you done? she said in a hoarse, weak wail.
Oh, what have you done . . .

They put her in the ambulance then and took her away.
In the building opposite that telephone was ringing again.

There was only one hospital she could go to, of course. I
walked, silent as memory, along those familiar corridors.
All was still. There were moments like that, I remembered
them, when things would go quiet suddenly, for no reason,
in the middle of the busiest morning, and calm would
spread like ether through the wards. A radio somewhere
was playing softly, and down in the kitchens a skivvy was
singing. They told me Adele was sleeping, that's how they
said it, she's sleeping now, as if sleep here were a special and
expensive kind of therapy. And they gave me a cold look.
But when I came back that evening she was awake, sitting
up straight in a white bed, like an eager bird tethered to a
perch, with her thin hands clenched on the counterpane and
her neck stretched out. The room smelled of milk and
violets, her smell. Felix was there, and Professor Kosok.
The professor sat with his legs crossed, drumming his
fingers on his knee and looking at the ceiling. I paused in the
doorway.

– Here's bonny sweet Robin, said Felix. What, no
sweetmeats for the fair maid, no flowers fresh with
dew?

Adele's eyes were feverishly lit, and she kept laughing.
– Look at this place, she said, what am I doing here, I'm
perfectly all right.

Her gaze slid past me, it would fix on nothing. There was an angry patch of red at the corner of her mouth, she scratched it with her fingernails, scratched and scratched. She was still in her slip, with her fur coat thrown over her shoulders. She had been pulling at her hair, it stuck out, blue-black and gleaming, like a tatter of feathers. Felix spoke to me behind his hand with mock solemnity.

– She is importunate, indeed distract.

He chuckled. Light of evening glowed in the window. Outside was the top of a brick wall, and a flat expanse of roof with a chimney like a ship's funnel, belching white smoke. The professor shifted on his chair and sighed.

– It's late, he said to no one in particular. I have to go.

But still he sat there, with eyes upcast, his fingers drumming, drumming. A moment passed, like something being carried carefully through our midst. Then Felix laughed again softly and said:

– Yes, boss, come on, it's time we went.

At the door the professor hesitated, pretending to search for something in his pockets. He frowned. Adele would not look at him. Felix gave him a playful shove, and winked at me over his shoulder, and then they were gone.

I watched the blown smoke outside. The evening sky was pale. In the distance I could see the faint outlines of mountains. Adele kept her face averted. I tried to touch her hand but she took it away, not hastily, but with firmness, like a child taking away a toy.

– I have no peace, you see, she said. No peace. And what will I do here?

She sighed, and shook her head, with an air of mild annoyance, as if all this were just something that had got in the way of other, infinitely more important matters that now would have to wait.

– I'm sorry, I said.

Distantly in the sky a great flock of birds soared and wheeled, dark flashing suddenly to light as a thousand wings turned as one. Icarus. Adele looked about her vaguely.

– They took away my cigarettes, she said. You'll have to bring me some.

And for the first time since I had come there she looked at me directly, with that fierce, strabismic stare.

– Won't you? she said. You'll have to . . .

The door behind me opened, I turned, and matron stopped on the threshold and looked at us.

Order, pattern, harmony. Press hard enough upon anything, upon everything, and the random would be resolved. I waited, impatient, in a state of grim elation. I had thrown out the accumulated impedimenta of years. I was after simplicity now, the pure, uncluttered thing. Everywhere were secret signs. The machine sang to me, for was not I too built on a binary code? One and zero, these were the poles. The rushings of spring shook my heart. I could not sleep, I wandered the brightening streets for hours, prey to a kind of joyless hilarity. I was in pain. When I lay down at last, exhausted, watching the sky, the fleeting clouds, a dull, grey ache would lodge in the pit of my stomach, like a grey rat, lodging there. At ashen twilight I would rise, my eyelids burning, and something thudding in my head, and set off for the hospital.

There too a frantic mood held sway. I would arrive in Adele's room and find her with Felix and Father Plomer, all three of them bright-eyed and breathless somehow, as if at the end of some wild romp. The priest was a frequent visitor, he would put his head around the door with a conspiratorial smile, and enter on tiptoe, plump and large in his black suit and embroidered stole, his glasses flashing. He clasped his hands and laughed, showing his white teeth and gold fillings. He was like a big awkward excited girl. He loved to be there. Let's have a little party! he would say, and he would get one of the kitchen girls to bring up a pot of tea and plates of bread and butter. Before he sat down he would remove his stole reverently and kiss it, closing his eyes briefly. Then he would lift his hands heavenwards and softly say:

– Ah, freedom!

Felix he treated with a sort of tremulous familiarity, prancing around him nervously and tittering at his jokes.

– Oh, you have a wicked wit, he would say. A wicked wit!

And Felix would look past the priest's shoulder and catch my eye, smiling, his thin lips stretched tight.

Adele sat up in our midst, with her stark white face and her fright of hair. She had changed her slip for a satin tea-gown with roses and birds, it made the room seem more than ever like an aviary. She laughed more and more too, but more and more her laughter sounded like the first

203

startled screeches of something that had blundered on widespread wings into a net. Her eyes grew dull, a faint, whitish film was spreading over the pupils. She complained about the light, it was not bright enough, but when the venetian blinds were drawn up, or another lamp was brought, she covered her face and turned away from the glare.

Outside her door after one of our visits Father Plomer hung back with an air of solemn excitement and spoke to Felix and me.

– I mean to save her, you know, he said. Oh yes, she's agreed to take instruction.

Felix reared back from the priest in wide-eyed wonder.

– Oi vay! he breathed, and put up a hand to hide the thin little mocking smirk he could not stifle.

Then for a while that romping air I used to find when I arrived in her room gave way to a tense, reverential atmosphere, in which something seemed to vibrate, as if a little bell had just stopped ringing. Once I even came upon them in the act of prayer, the priest down on one knee, a hand to his forehead and his missal open, and Adele lying back on the pillows with her hands folded on her breast and her eyes cast upwards, wan and waxen in her satin gown, like a picture of a drowned maiden laid out on the flower-strewn bank of a brook. But it did not last. One day she snatched the prayerbook from him with a laugh and flung it across the room, and although he hung about in the corridor with a wounded look she would not consent to see him any more.

– Don't worry, padre, Felix said to him jauntily, she'll find her own way to the light.

That night she was gay, she sat with her ankles crossed under the covers and an ashtray in her lap. She had put on lipstick and mascara, and painted her fingernails scarlet. She waved her cigarette about, fluttering her lashes and pouting like a vamp.

– He tried to put his hand under my clothes, she said. Imagine!

Felix fairly whooped.

– Oh my, oh my! he cried, clutching himself. So much for salvation, eh?

When he was gone she sat and plucked at the bedclothes, frowning. She would not meet my eye. She picked up a magazine and flipped through it distractedly.

– Listen, she said, you'll have to get me something. That bitch will only give me that stuff, that method stuff, what do you call it, it's no good.

She ceased turning the gaudy pages and sat quite still, her head bowed. There was silence. She dropped her cigarette into the ashtray and watched with narrowed eyes the thin blue plume of smoke pouring upwards.

– I can't, I said. How can I.

For a moment she said nothing, and did not stir, it was as if she had not heard.

– Yes, she said quietly. That's what he says, too. And then he laughs.

She looked up at me and tried to smile. The sore patch at the corner of her painted mouth was raw. Her lower lip was trembling.

– She gives you things, doesn't she? she said. Pills, those things? You can ask her. You can say it's for yourself.

She struggled up, overturning the ashtray, and knelt on

the edge of the bed and clasped her arms around my neck
and pressed her trembling mouth on mine. She began to
cry. Lipstick, smoke, salt tears. That taste, I can taste it
still.

– I'll let you do it to me, she moaned. Everything,
everything you want. Everything . . .

STOLE IT FOR HER. I knew where to look, what to take. Matron was not at her desk, the key to the dispensary was in her drawer. I walked upstairs. It was teatime, no one paid me any heed. In a hospital even I could go unnoticed. I locked the dispensary door behind me. How quiet it was there suddenly, like being underwater, amid all those shelves of greenish glass, those phials brimming with sleep. I found what I had come for, but still I lingered, leaning by the window. It was a gusty twilight. A sky full of wreckage flowed overhead in silence. Down in the grounds a cherry tree whipped and shuddered, its fallen blossoms washing in waves back and forth over the grey grass. How many moments had I known like this, when everything altered somehow, like a carousel coming briefly to a stop, and I saw once again with weary eyes the thing that had been there all the time. I pressed my forehead to the glass. To stay here, to stay here forever, like this. To have it over, finally.

· · ·

She was up pacing the floor, holding herself tightly in her arms. She flew at me, where had I been! I handed her the tiny plastic ampoules. She thrust them into a pocket of her gown and stood a moment motionless, with a sort of vacant grin, gazing at nothing. Then she frowned. No, she muttered, no, the room wasn't safe, there was no lock on the door, anyone could walk in. Besides, her things were not here, she had hidden them. She paced again, talking to herself, one hand stuck in her hair and the other tearing at the sore on her mouth. Then she halted, nodding.

– There'll be no one there, she said. There's never anyone there at this time, it will be all right.

She clutched my arm.

– Yes, she said, yes, it will be all right.

It strikes me suddenly how like cloisters were those corridors, with their arched ceilings, their statues and their lilies, that quiet that was not quite silence. She hurried ahead of me, keeping to the wall, a barefoot wraith. She led me to the chapel. It was a little vaulted cell hung with flags and pennants and holy pictures in big brown frames. A stained-glass window, from which the last light was fading, depicted the assumption of the Virgin in pinks and gaudy blues. There were daffodils on the miniature altar. A brass oil lamp with a ruby-red globe was suspended from the ceiling on a heavy chain. The place, festooned and dim, had a jaded, vaguely sybaritic air, like the tent of a desert chieftain. There was a smell of wood and wax. The silence here too was somehow murmurous, as if thronged with lingering echoes. Adele reached behind a picture of skewered St Sebastian and brought out a plastic bag that had been taped with sticking plaster to the back of the frame. We stood for a moment in the holy hush, with our heads together, admiring her treasures. There was a little bottle and a spoon, a rubber dropper, and a disposable syringe, its needle bent, that she had salvaged from a waste bin. I was thinking of another occasion, when we had stood like this, in each other's warmth, our breath mingling. Outside the wind was blowing. Her hands trembled. The wounded saint considered us with his level, sad, lascivious gaze.

She knelt at the step in front of the altar to blend her brew, while I sat on a bench and watched. She worked with loving, rapt attention, biting her lip and frowning, forgetting herself. I hardly knew her, kneeling there, transfigured, lost in her task, a votive priestess. Now and then she had to stop and wait for the shaking in her hands to subside, and looked about her dimly, with unseeing eyes. She lit a stump of penny candle and set it on the step and warmed the mixture in the spoon. Then she sat back on her heels and rolled the sleeve of her gown to the shoulder. Her naked arm glimmered in the fading light. She found a vein, and squeezed and squeezed until it stood up, plump and purple, gorged with blood. At first the needle would not penetrate, and she prodded and pushed, making a faint mewling sound and arching her back. Then suddenly the tip went in, and the swollen skin slid up around it, like a tiny pouting mouth, drawing the fine steel shaft deep inside itself, and she pressed the plunger slowly, while the pulsing vein sucked and sucked, and at last she leaned her head back, her eyelids fluttering, and exhaled a long, shivering sigh.

I knelt on the cold floor and held her. She stared at me

sightlessly. Her hand, still holding the syringe, lay limply beside her on the step. I crushed the chill silk stuff of her gown in my hands.

– You promised, I said. You promised.

I lifted her up and walked her to the door, and made her stand with her back to it so that no one could come in. She put one arm across my shoulders, and with the other held my head in a fierce embrace, grinding her chin into my jaw. Her thighs were cold. I listened in vague wonder to my own hoarse quickening gasps. The back of her head beat dully against the thick oak door. She was laughing, or crying, I don't know which.

– You'll get more for me, won't you, she said into my ear. Say it, say you'll get more.

– Yes, I said, yes.

But I did not have to get it, I had it already, enough to keep her going for weeks, it was still in my pocket, enough to keep us both going, for weeks.

And so at the same time evening after evening we came there to the chapel, and I gave her that day's ration of peace, and in return she opened her gown and briefly held me, gasping, pressed to her shivering flesh. I recall the quiet around us, the light dying in that garish window, and the smell of the place, like the smell of coffins, and the vague clamour of teatime outside in the wards, a noise from another world. Afterwards we would sit for a long time together in the dim glow of the flickering altar lamp, as another day died and night came on. Sometimes an old woman in a dressing-gown would creep in and kneel for a while, sighing and mumbling, with her face in her hands. She paid us no heed, perhaps she never noticed us. It was May, the month of Mary, fresh flowers were placed on the altar every day, daffodils, and tulips, and lilies of the valley. Adele sat with head bowed and her hands in her lap, so still she seemed hardly to breathe. I told her about numbers, how they worked, how simple they were, how pure. I do not know if she was even listening. I told her too about that moment on the mountain, how it had come to me afresh, with more weight than ever, that under the chaos of things a hidden order endures. A kind of rapture thickened in my throat, I gagged on it as if on grief. She leaned her shoulder wearily against mine.

– I have to get out of this place, she said. Help me.

A bell was ringing, they would come in soon to say the rosary. I rose to go. She looked up at me, out of her dark, dazed eyes.

– Help me, she said.

Felix listened to me, he understood. That's it, he said, that's it! smiling and nodding, urging me on. To know, to do, to delve into the secret depths of things, wasn't that what he had always urged on me? And now he would help me. He had contacts, he had influence. There were people other than the professor, there were other machines, too, bigger, and better, oh yes, yes, he would show me! I liked to listen to him talk like this, it set up a kind of excited hum inside me that had alarm in it, and presentiment, and dark pleasure.

And if now and then I looked up unexpectedly and caught him watching me with a merry eye, smiling that artful smile of his, well, I didn't care.

In the afternoon sometimes I walked about the city with him. We went to the zoo, one of his favourite haunts. He found everything irresistibly funny there. He would stand in front of the tiger's cage, or in the torpid gloom of the alligator house, and fairly split his sides. The animals in their turn watched him with what seemed to me a puzzled, wary eye. Oh look, look! he would cry, in a transport, clutching my arm and pointing a trembling finger at a baboon picking at its purple arse, or a hippo trying to mount its mate.

– What a strange old world, all the same, he said, that has such monsters in it, eh, Caliban?

He met people there, they would step out from behind a tree, or lower a newspaper and look at him with a humid stare. There was something about them, an air of tension and vague torment, that fitted with the place. They might have been peering through invisible bars. When he spotted them he would laugh softly to himself and walk over rapidly and talk to them, keeping his back to me. He never referred to these encounters afterwards, but fell into step beside me again and blandly took up talking where he had left off. But some days I noticed him looking about with a watchful eye, and a trace of strain crept into his smile, and he kept to open ground.

– If you ever have to look for me, he said, you know where I'll be, don't you?

We were walking by an ornamental lake. The day was overcast, the air a sheen of damp pearl. He was eating a pink ice-cream cone, and kicking idly at the ducks crowding the churned mud of the water margin.

– I mean, he said, if you can't find me, if I'm not around. When matters become complicated, a period of withdrawal is the best thing, I find.

He glanced at me and grinned. A black swan sailed past us in silence, with its chaste, bashful mien. The ducks gabbled. He tossed the last of his ice-cream into their midst and there was uproar. On a little island in the lake a pair of monkeys swung and chattered in the branches of a dead tree.

– We should stick together, Felix said. We're two of a kind, you and me.

He linked his arm in mine then, and we went through the gate and up the hill to the bus stop. The city was below us, crouched under a lowering sky. We were stopped in traffic by the river when the rain came on, rattling against the side of the bus. It ceased as abruptly as it had begun, and a pale wash of sunlight fell across the rooftops and the shining spires, and at a great height a solitary white bird soared against a bruise-coloured wall of cloud. How innocent it all was, how unconcerned, I remember it, the drenched light, the spires, that bird, like a dreamy background, done by an apprentice, perhaps, while in front horses plunge and blackamoors roll their eyes, and a poor wretch is dying tacked to a tree.

In Chandos Street we found Liz huddled on the steps outside the front door. When we approached her she flinched and put up her arms to protect her face. There was a livid bruise under her eye, and her lower lip was split and caked with blood. She would not stand up, but cowered against the door with her knees pressed to her chest. I knelt beside her, but she turned her face away from me with a sob. Felix stood before her with his hands in his pockets, tapping one foot.

– Tony being impetuous again, is he? he said. That boy is so excitable.

Liz mumbled something. One of her front teeth had been knocked out, it was hard to understand her.

– Come again? Felix said, leaning down with a hand cupped to his ear.

– He's gone! she cried.

There was silence, save for her muffled sobs. It was growing dark in the street. Felix considered her pensively, jingling coins in his pocket.

– Gone? he said softly. How do you mean, gone?

She squeezed her eyes shut, but the tears kept coming. Her lip had begun to bleed again. She held herself by the shoulders, trembling.

– They were waiting for us on the corner, she said. They made him go with them.

Felix looked up and down the street, then leaned down to her again, with his hands on his knees, and smiled.

– They, now, he said. Who were they, exactly?

She shook her head.

– Ah, he said. Strangers. Tell me, my dear, would you say they were, perhaps, seafaring gentlemen? Yes?

He glanced at me, still smiling.

– Well well, he said, a pair of jolly tars, no less. I wonder, now, who they can have been.

He skipped down the steps and stood on the pavement, peering about the street again, more carefully this time.

Then he came back. He examined Liz's face closely, squatting on his heels in front of her and shaking his head.

– You don't look at all well, he said, do you know that? Not at all well.

She watched him warily, snuffling, running a hand through her matted, ash-coloured hair. He smiled at her and lifted his eyebrows, holding his head to one side.

– Tell you what, he said, how about a treat, to make it all better. What do you think? Wouldn't that be nice?

He brought out from an inside pocket a tiny square plastic envelope and held it up for her to see, wagging it gaily under her nose. At once she sprang at him and tried to snatch it, but he drew back, grinning.

– Ah ah! he said. First, a question. What did they want, precisely, these sailor laddies?

She watched the little envelope, licking her broken lips.

– You, she said. It was you they were looking for.

He stared in mock astonishment, clapping a hand to his heart.

– Me? he gasped. Me? Good gracious!

He laughed, and rose from where he had been squatting and turned away from her. With a cry she scrambled after him on her knees, clutching at the tail of his mackintosh. He paused.

– Oh, your fizz-bag, yes, he said. Here.

He tossed the envelope on the step. She grabbed it, and clawed it open, and with her fingers drew down her swollen lower lip and shook the contents into the crevice between lip and gums. Then she crawled back and sat down at the door again, hugging her knees to her chest. She was crying, we could hear her as we walked away into the dusk.

At a phone box on the corner of the square Felix stopped. He cradled the receiver under his chin, holding the door open with his knee and winking at me as he spoke.

– Yes, Chandos Street, yes. I think she must have taken something, she looks very . . . What's that? Me, officer? Oh, just a citizen, doing his duty. Bye bye, now.

He let the door bang shut behind him, and turned up the collar of his coat and rolled his eyes.

– The plot thickens, he said, eh, Watson?

It was in the final editions, foul play down the docks, the body of a young man taken from the river, severe injuries to head and face, unrecognizable. Police were keeping an open mind.

THE CITY I HAD THOUGHT I knew became transfigured now. Fear altered everything. I scanned the streets with a sort of passion, under the glare of it things grew flustered somehow, seemed to shrink away from me, as if stricken with shyness. They had never been noticed before, or at least not like this, with this fierce, concupiscent scrutiny. I saw pursuers everywhere, no, not pursuers, that's not it, that's too strong. But nothing was innocent any more. The squares, the avenues, the little parks, all my old haunts, they were a façade now, behind which lurked a lewd, malignant presence. Panic smouldered in me like a chronic fever, ready to flare up at the smallest fright. Walking along the street I would suddenly speed up my steps, until I was flying along, head down, heart hammering, my breath coming in little cries, yet when I stopped at last, exhausted, and looked behind me, there was never anything there, only a sense in general of low, gloating laughter. Twilight I found especially alarming, that hour of shadows and dim perspectives, I fled from it into the fluorescent sanctuary of the white room, where everything seemed its own source of light, and surfaces were impassive, without deceptive depths, and the atmosphere was neutral and inert, like a thin, colourless gas.

There was little to do there now. The transmissions from abroad had ceased altogether. The professor paced and scowled in furious silence, a man betrayed. The telephone was left permanently off the hook. Some nights he did not appear at all, and Leitch and I were left alone in a fraught, uneasy intimacy. Leitch was restless too, he prowled about softly in his slippers, his hands stuck in the drooping pockets of his trousers. No matter where he was in the room I fancied I could hear him breathing. He told me his jokes, and offered me choice tidbits from his foodbag. I had preferred the old animosity to this somehow menacing warmth. I felt as if I were holding on to a tether in the dark, at any moment what was at the other end might rear up and savage me. He tended the machine now with a kind of frenzied vigilance, watching over it like a thwarted, jealous parent, cursing it, kicking it, throwing crusts of bread at it. The thing suffered these affronts in silence, dully, its attention somehow averted, as if it were thinking about something else entirely. It maddened him, its imperturbability, its complete, ponderous, irredeemable stupidity.

– It knows nothing, the professor said, nothing it has not been told.

Leitch drew his great head down into his shoulders, his bruised dark gaze wandering here and there about the room.

– Yes, he said bitterly under his breath, just like us.

One night he came up behind me in the lavatory and put

his arms around my waist. I tried to free myself, and we tussled briefly, rolling from side to side in a sort of laborious hornpipe. We staggered out the door into the corridor, where our grunts and gasps echoed like the sounds of a real fight. I got an elbow into his chest at last and gave him a tremendous push. He fell back, winded, and leaned against the wall with his mouth open and a hand pressed to his breastbone. His cravat was twisted under one ear, and he had lost a slipper. He glowered at me with a smeared eye.

– What's up with you! he said. He told me . . .

He paused.

– He told you what, I said. He told you a lie.

I wanted to kick him, I could almost feel my foot sinking into that soft belly, could see him on all-fours puking up his sticky supper. I was angry not because he had laid hands on me, but because I knew that now I could not be there any more.

– Look at you, he was saying, Jesus, what a freak.

He turned his face to the wall and wept, in sorrow and in rage, his chubby shoulders shaking. I went out into the night. The air was black and wet, foghorns were blaring in the bay. The building towered above me, seeming to topple slowly in the drifting mist, all windows dark. No one was about. I walked away. Another sanctuary was gone.

Adele sat on a chair beside her bed, brushing her hair with slow, stiff strokes. She was wearing an old dressing-gown tied with a frayed cord. Her face, bare of make-up, was pale and blurred, as if she had scrubbed at it so hard the features had become worn. She gazed before her dully. Father Plomer stood at the window, facing the room, with his arms folded and his head thrown back. Behind him the sun shone on the flat roof and the smoking funnel, and far away a tiny aeroplane glinted, crawling athwart a clear blue sky. His face was in shadow, the silvery lenses of his spectacles gleaming like coins. Matron was there too, standing behind Adele, quite still, and leaning forward a little, in that way she had, her arms hanging. They seemed posed, the three of them, as if they had been placed just so, for a group portrait. Adele did not look at me, as if she did not know that I was there. I had brought cigarettes for her. Matron put out a hand silently and took them.

– Adele has given up smoking, Father Plomer said. Haven't you, my dear? A new life. She's going to lead a new life.

And he smiled, blank-eyed and bland. Adele went on pulling the brush through her hair, stroke by stroke. Matron continued to look at me for a moment, then turned away, for the last time.

When I went to the chapel that evening Adele was not there. I was not surprised. She was in her room, asleep, stranded among the tangled sheets as if a wave had deposited her there. I sat for a while in the stillness, watching her. It was bright yet outside, but the blind was shut, a grey half-light suffused the room. Twilight, her hour. Hers too that lost, wan, tender shade of grey. Her lips were open, one hand lay on the pillow beside her cheek. I put the ampoules into the pocket of her dressing-gown and went out quietly and shut the door behind me.

The bus swayed and pitched along the narrow roads, wallowing on the bends, the gears roaring. Trees advanced at a rush into the headlights, their branches thrown up in astonishment, then plunged past us into the darkness again. I was in the seat by the door, near the driver, a lean, pale, taciturn man who sat with his bony knees splayed, turning the big flat steering wheel with a rolling motion of his arms, as if he were hauling in a rope. At the stops he would lean forward and rest his elbows on the wheel, his wrists crossed, and suck his teeth and gaze out at the road. We went through a village, and halted at a dark crossroads where an old man with a crutch got on. He paused on the step and looked at me, panting, his old mouth open toothlessly at one side. We climbed for a long time, then bounced across an open plateau, I could see faint stars low down to right and left, and a gibbous moon perched on the point of a far peak. Sometimes too, when the road wound back on itself, I caught a glimpse of the lights of the city far off in the distance behind us. Then we rolled down into a hollow and stopped, and the driver looked at me.

Different air, and the smell of pines, and a crisp wind, and stars. I watched the bus depart, the rear-lights weaving slowly up the side of the hill. Then quiet, and the sound of water. A dim light burned over the door of the pub, and there was a light in the dirty window too. I walked across the gravel. He must have heard the bus stopping, or maybe he was watching from the window. He hung back in the darkness of the doorway until he had got a good look at me, then he came forward with a hand lifted in greeting.

– Ah, Melmoth, he said softly. We've been expecting you.

When I think of that second visit to the Goat I imagine a long, low, turf-brown tavern with oil lamps and glinting copper mugs, and hams and things hanging from the rafters. The picture only needs a pot-boy in an apron and a merry old codger with curly side-whiskers and a meerschaum warming his shanks in the inglenook. Where do they come from, these fantasies? When I entered first the place seemed deserted. Fat Dan stood behind the bar, picking his side teeth delicately with the nail of a little finger. He wore a shirt without a collar, and a green sleeveless pullover, tight as a harness, that stopped halfway down his belly. He greeted me with a large, slow wink, involving less the closing of an eye than the opening sideways of his mouth.

– A hot toddy, Dan, for the traveller, Felix said.

We sat on stools at the bar. As I became accustomed to the gloom I picked out a few other customers here and there, big silent countrymen in caps and long, buttonless overcoats, whose eyes veered away like fish when they met mine. Felix watched me as I supped the steaming liquor. He was wearing plus-fours and argyle socks, and a cloth cap with a button in the crown.

– I'm glad you've come down, he said, really I am. It gets awfully monotonous here.

I told him Tony's body had been found. He put a finger quickly to his lips and cast a meaning glance in Dan's direction.

– Yes, he said quietly, I saw that too. Most sad. I was shocked, I can tell you.

I said nothing. He studied me with a rueful little grin.

– I say, he said, I hope you don't think I was to blame, do you? I didn't lead them to Chandos Street, after all. It wasn't me they followed.

He took out his tobacco tin and lit up a butt, and watched me through the smoke, still smiling.

– Now don't get down in the dumps, he said. It wasn't anybody's fault. It was just a sort of accident.

– An accident, I said.

He tittered.

– But of course, he said, you don't believe in accidents, do you, I forgot. Everything is a part of the pattern. Well, perhaps poor Anthony's demise is indeed a link in some grand plan, or plot, but that still doesn't mean that anyone is to blame, now does it?

He smoked in silence for a while, brooding, then laid a finger on my wrist and said:

– And you're not to worry, either. Just remember, ships must sail, eventually.

– They come back, too, I said.

He laughed.

– Oh, yes, he said. *Die ewige Wiederkunft*, eh?

Fat Dan approached, and leaned a forearm on the bar and

inclined his head towards me in a confidential manner. Would I be wanting to stay? he wondered.

– Any friend of Mr Felix is welcome here, he said, breathing warm sincerity and smiling.

He led me up a narrow stairs, his great shiny backside swaying ahead of me. I remember him holding a candle, but surely that's another fantasy. At the back his hair was shaved to the top of his head, where a boyish little lick stuck up. His neck was a big wad of red fat with bristles. On the landing he paused, panting softly, and looked at me with a sort of ogling grin, as though there were some faintly scandalous secret unspoken between us. He nodded back down the stairs, in the direction of the bar, and said:

– He's a queer card, all the same though, what?

He showed me into a tiny room with a low, sagging ceiling, a single small square window, and an enormous brass bed. The wallpaper, embossed with flower shapes, had once been white, but was now a sticky amber colour, it seemed to have been varnished. The wainscoting was brown, the paint combed to look like grained oak. Dan stood gazing a moment in the doorway with a solemn air.

– This used to be the mammy's room, one time, he said quietly.

He sighed, and more quietly still he added:

– Before she fell into flesh.

When he was gone I put out the light and sat on the bed in the dark for a long time. The moon was higher now, riding in a corner of the window. I could see the vague shapes of pines outside, swaying in the wind, and beyond them, far off on the sides of the surrounding hills, the little lights of cottages and farms dotted here and there, frail beacons in the midst of so much darkness. I heard the last of the drinkers leave and tramp away along the hill road, and then the sounds of Dan locking up for the night. A dog barked for a while in the distance, listlessly. My scars ached.

What was I thinking about?

Nothing. Numbers.

Nothing.

We tramped the hills for hours, Felix and I, day after day. The weather was windy and bright, the last of spring, the flushed air rife with the singing of larks. It made me giddy, to be for so long up so high. Everything tended skywards here, as if gravity had somehow lost its hold. White clouds would fly up from behind a granite peak, billowing upwards into the zenith. There was nothing to hold on to, all around us as far as the horizon stretched the browns and flat greens of bracken and bog. Then suddenly we would come to a turn in the path and find ourselves on the edge of a stony crater, with a steel-grey lake far below us and a little puff of pale cloud floating in midair.

– Ah, wonderful! Felix cried. Doesn't it make you feel like something out of Caspar David Friedrich?

He laid a hand on his heart and breathed deep, smiling for bliss, his eyes closed and nostrils flared. He was wearing his plus-fours and his cap, and carried a tall spiked stick. I watched shadows streaming like water down the far flank of the crater.

– What did you say about me to Leitch? I said.

He opened his eyes wide and stared at me in exaggerated startlement. Then he broke into silent laughter, the tip of his tongue coming out and quickly vanishing again.

– Why? he said slyly. Worried for your reputation, are you?

– That was a place to be, I said. Now I can't go there any more.

At that he laughed out loud, striking his stick on the stony ground.

– Boo hoo! he said, sneering. Listen, that place is finished, you know it. They thought the old boy was doing something brilliant, until they found out he was using their precious machine to prove that nothing can be proved.

He walked to the edge of the path and lifted hieratic arms above the abyss, thrusting the alpenstock aloft.

– O world in chaos! he intoned. Blind energy, spinning in the void! All turns, returns. Thus spake the prophet.

He came back, hobbling and wheezing, a bent old geezer now, using his stick as a crutch, and squinted up into my face.

– Here's place enough, and time, he said.

Wind swooped past us down the slope and wrinkled the steely surface of the lake. The sunlight sparkled. He took my arm and walked me along slowly, with priestly solicitude.

– Put yourself in my hands, he said. I have high hopes for you, you know. Really, I have.

We rounded another turn in the path and came out on a rocky ledge. From here we could see in the distance a dense blue smear of smoke that was the city. Below us was the pub, and the road winding away. He squeezed my arm against his ribs.

— What do you say, eh? he said. Think of the times we've had, you and me. And think of the future.

I went ahead of him, down the side of the hill. On the bridge over the little stream behind the pub I paused to swallow a pill. He stopped a pace behind me, with his head on one side, smiling faintly and scraping in the dust with his stick.

— And behold, he said, angels came and ministered unto him.

I left that night. Felix and I waited in the bar for the time when the bus would arrive. The setting sun blazed briefly in the window, then the shadows gathered. Fat Dan was offended that I would not stay. He wiped the top of the counter with slow strokes of a dishcloth, glancing at me soulfully now and then. In the end, though, curiosity overcame his sense of umbrage, and he edged closer and closer, wielding the cloth in ever narrowing sweeps, and spoke at last.

— Them burns, he said, did you get acid on you, or what?

Felix rolled his eyes.

— It's the mark of Cain, Dan, he said.

I told my tale. Dan was enthralled, he had never heard such a thing, grafts, tinfoil bandages, all that. He folded his arms on the counter and leaned his plump breasts on his arms and gazed at me in awe, as if it were some marvellous feat I had performed.

— Holy God, he said, you've been through the wars, all right.

– And now he's banished, in the land of Nod, Felix said.

Dan paid him no heed, but glanced about the bar, as if there might be someone who would overhear, and leaned closer to me with a portentous air.

– Come here, he said, come on here, now.

He took down a big iron key from a hook behind him, and lifted the flap of the counter and stood back to let me enter. I looked at Felix. He shrugged.

– Go ahead, he said. There are some things even I don't know.

Dan led the way through a door behind the bar into a narrow, dim passageway with cluttered shelves and crates of bottles on the floor. There was a musty smell of apples and of clay. For a moment I felt I had been here before, long ago. We came to another door. Dan paused with the key in the keyhole.

– I knew you weren't like them others he brings up here, he said. I knew you were different.

And he smiled and winked.

The room was small, and filled with things. A banked-up coke fire throbbed in the grate. By the fire, in a vast armchair, a vast woman sat. She had a great round head, like the head of a stone statue, and ragged sparse white hair. Her bloated face glistened in the glare of the coals like a glazed mask that had begun to melt. She wore a sort of gown of some heavy shiny black stuff, and a knitted jacket draped over her shoulders like a cape.

– This, Dan said, is Mammy.

Out of that swollen mask two tiny glittering eyes fixed on me an avid, unwavering stare. She did not speak. A window at the far side of the room looked out on to a scrubby bit of garden where a few hens were scratching in the dirt. The jagged tops of the pines stood stark as black teeth against the sky, as if a huge mouth were closing slowly around us. The hour was growing dark. Dan brought a chair for me and I sat down. Mammy smelled of peppermint, and of things that had been worn for too long next the skin. Each breath she took was a deep, harsh draught, it shuddered into her, subsiding, and then she was still for a moment, until the next one started. Dan sat down beside me, rubbing his palms on his knees, his big face shining.

– There's not many are let come in here, he said loudly. Isn't that so, Mammy?

He smiled sheepishly, gazing at her proudly, as if somehow she, not he, were the offspring. She ignored him, he might not have been there. Her hand lay on the armrest beside me, stuck like a stopper into the end of her fat arm. Her face was almost featureless, nose, mouth, cheeks, all had melted into shapeless fat. Only the eyes remained, undimmed. Since I came in her gaze had not shifted from me for an instant, it was at once remote and intent, as if she were not used to looking at human creatures. The air thudded softly, heavy with heat. The room crowded around us. There was a table, cabinets, cupboards, a brass coal scuttle, a sofa with its stuffing coming out, two china dogs eyeing each other on the mantelpiece, a porcelain ballerina in a tutu made of real lace, a silver cake-stand, a bookcase without books, a glass globe with an alpine scene inside it and stuff that would make a snowstorm, a bow of crimson satin saved from a chocolate box, a pair of toby jugs, a ship under full sail in a bottle, a coloured picture of Mary, the Mother of God, with a dagger piercing her heart.

Dan was talking away, but I was not listening. The darkness deepened, the fire shone red. I wanted to leave, to get away, yet could not, a kind of voluptuous lethargy had taken hold of me, my limbs were leaden, like flasks filled with heavy liquid. And it seemed to me that somehow I had always been here, and somehow would remain here always, among Mammy's things, with her little unrelenting eye fixed on me. She signified something, no, she signified nothing. She had no meaning. She was simply there. And would be there, waiting, in that fetid little room, forever.

The bus was late. Felix and I paced up and down outside the pub. The night was clear and starry. Felix was pensive, whistling softly through his teeth. He didn't know why I was going, he said, why I wouldn't wait a few days more. He would be leaving too, then. We might have gone together. He glanced at me sideways, trying to make out my expression in the darkness.

My expression.

– Can't tempt you, eh? he said. Well, there'll be another time.

I gazed away up the road. He touched my arm lightly.

– Oh, yes, he said, there's always another time.

Then he walked off, laughing, into the night.

The hill road gleamed, the pines sighed, the light from the lamp over the door of the pub shivered in the wind. Absence, absence, the forlorn weight of all that was not there.

THE LILAC WAS IN bloom in the hospital grounds. The first frail venturers of the season were out in their slippers and their dressing-gowns, holding up their shocked ashen faces to the sun. On the roof gay puffs of white smoke streamed away in the wind, they made the building seem for a moment a great ship bounding through the blue. The entrance hall was a glare of light. A sparrow had got in somehow, and was beating its wings against the glass in the corner of a high window, I can hear it still, that tiny, frantic commotion. They stopped me at the desk.

– Are you a relative? they said.

A shaft of sunlight thronged with dust-motes stood aslant the stairs, like a pillar falling and falling.

Mother.

I walked down a corridor, waited in a room. There was a table, plastic chairs, a vase of dried flowers. Time passed, an age. I was there, and not there. At last Father Plomer arrived, and stood before me with his soft hands clasped. He was not wearing his spectacles, without them his eyes had a raw, damaged look. He shook his head, as if over some mild disappointment, or some inclemency of the weather.

– I'm sorry, he said.

Icarus. Icarus.

Full is the cup.

I wanted to see her room. The bed had been stripped, the waste bin emptied, the locker door stood open. And yet, for me, she was there, there in all that was missing. Had it ever been otherwise? I leaned my head at the window, watching the smoke on the roof, the little clouds, the far, shadowy hills. A frozen sea was breaking up inside me. Father Plomer paced softly, his leather soles creaking.

– She was found in the chapel, you know, he said. I take that as a great sign, that she would go there, to be at peace.

He paused and looked at me, with that naked, groping gaze, then paced again, creaking.

– Of course, the question is, he said, where did she get that awful, awful stuff, and so much of it. The powers that be have their suspicions, and if they prove right, a certain person, I can tell you, will be losing her position here, and very soon, at that.

Again he glanced at me, with a meaning look, and nodded slowly once. Do I imagine it, or did he rub his hands?

I found Professor Kosok at the flat in Chandos Street. He was sitting by the window in the kitchen, in his overcoat and hat. One fist lay clenched before him on the table. His eyes were red, fat tears rolled down the greasy sides of his nose. They had given him her things in a plastic bag: her handbag, her fur coat, her flowered tea-gown. He looked at me wearily.

– Where is your order now? he said.

She was his daughter, did I mention that?

I walked through the bedrooms at the back. How grandly the sun dreamed here, falling down through the great windows, light from another time. I stood and wept. Summer! The garden was in blossom. A pigeon landed on the sill, spoke softly, and flew away again.

When I left I took her syringe with me, in its velvet case, as a keepsake.

A part of me, too, had died. I woke up one morning and found I could no longer add together two and two. Something had given way, the ice had shattered. Things crowded in, the mere things themselves. One drop of water plus one drop of water will not make two drops, but one. Two oranges and two apples do not make four of some new synthesis, but remain stubbornly themselves. Oh, I don't say I had not thought of all this before, only that now I could not think of anything else. About numbers I had known everything, and understood nothing.

I lost the black notebook, misplaced it somewhere, or threw it away, I don't know. Have I not made a black book of my own?

Grief, of course, and guilt. I shall not go into it. Pain too, but not so much as before, and every day a little less. My face is almost mended, one morning I'll wake up and not recognize myself in the mirror. A new man. I stay away from the hospital. What is there for me there, any more? I want no protectors now. I want to be, to be, what, I don't know. Naked. Flayed. A howling babe, waving furious fists. I don't know.

Have I tied up all the ends? Even an invented world has its rules, tedious, absurd perhaps, but not to be gainsaid.

Sometimes still I have the feeling, I think I'll never lose it, that I am being followed. More than once, as well, I have turned in the street at the sight of a flash of red hair, a face slyly smiling among the faceless ones. Is it my imagination? Was it ever anything else? He'll be back, in one form or another, there's no escaping him. I have begun to work again, tentatively. I have gone back to the very start, to the simplest things. Simple! I like that. It will be different this time, I think it will be different. I won't do as I used to, in the old days. No. In future, I will leave things, I will try to leave things, to chance.